EIGHT CYLINDERS

JASON PARENT

Let the world know:
#IGotMyCLPBook!

Crystal Lake Publishing
www.CrystalLakePub.com

Copyright © 2020 Jason Parent
All Rights Reserved

Be sure to sign up for our newsletter and receive a free eBook: http://eepurl.com/xfuKP

ISBN: 978-1-64669-306-1

Edited by:
Gwedolyn Nix

Cover Art:
Ben Baldwin—www.benbaldwin.co.uk

Layout:
Lori Michelle—www.theauthorsalley.com

Proofread by:
Kat Nava
James Tucker

This is a work of fiction. Names, characters, businesses, places, events and incidents are either the products of the authors' imagination or used in a fictitious manner. Any resemblance to actual persons, living or dead, or actual events is purely coincidental.

No part of this publication may be reproduced, stored in a retrieval system, or transmitted in any form or by any means, without the prior permission in writing of the publisher, nor be otherwise circulated in any form of binding or cover than that in which it is published and without a similar condition including this condition being imposed on the subsequent purchaser.

WELCOME
TO ANOTHER

CRYSTAL LAKE PUBLISHING
CREATION

Join today at www.crystallakepub.com & www.patreon.com/CLP

Welcome to another Crystal Lake Publishing creation.

Thank you for supporting independent publishing and small presses. You rock, and hopefully you'll quickly realize why we've become one of the world's leading publishers of Dark and Speculative Fiction. We have some of the world's best fans for a reason, and hopefully we'll be able to add you to that list really soon. Be sure to sign up for our newsletter to receive some free eBooks, as well as info on new releases, special offers, and so much more.

**Welcome to Crystal Lake Publishing—
Tales from the Darkest Depths.**

OTHER TITLES BY THE AUTHOR:

The Apocalypse Strain
What Hides Within
Victoria (What Hides Within Book 2)
Hearing Evil
They Feed
A Life Removed
People of the Sun
Wrathbone and Other Stories
Where Wolves Run
Unseemly
Seeing Evil

OTHER NOVELLAS BY CRYSTAL LAKE PUBLISHING:

Hollow Heart by Ben Eads
Every Foul Spirit by William Gorman
The Pale White by Chad Lutzke
A Season in Hell by Kenneth W. Cain
Quiet Places: A Novella of Cosmic Folk Horror by Jasper Bark
The Final Reconciliation by Todd Keisling
Run to Ground by Jasper Bark
Devourer of Souls by Kevin Lucia
Apocalyptic Montessa and Nuclear Lulu: A Tale of Atomic Love by Mercedes M. Yardley
Wind Chill by Patrick Rutigliano
Little Dead Red by Mercedes M. Yardley
Sleeper(s) by Paul Kane

CHAPTER 1

SEBASTIAN "SEB" MCCALISTER shook the mini Magic 8 Ball he'd plucked from Charlie Ling's eye. "Are we going to die today?"

Words bubbled to its surface. *Signs point to yes.*

Seb scoffed. *They certainly seem to.* Bullets flew over his head as he and his longtime partner in crime, Carlo Messina, crouched behind a parked car in the middle of a mostly empty department store parking lot. At just after two o'clock in the morning, the store was closed, and the lot should have been dead. Lucky for Seb, at least a few people, besides Ling's men, had parked there, their cars offering cover. Perhaps the store's cleaners or a security guard or two hid somewhere nearby while a small war ensued around their vehicles. Seb hoped they would stay hidden, stay safe even if it meant they would probably be calling the cops. He and Carlo crouched behind a brown Impala that took more bullets than a blindfolded man before a firing squad. The Jeep at their backs had taken a dozen shots itself.

Ling had them pinned behind that car, and all Seb could think about was how thankful he was that they hadn't sought cover behind his baby, a brand-spanking-new, granite-crystal metallic painted Dodge Charger SRT Hellcat he'd boosted a little over a month ago but had already fallen in love with. He loved only three things in the world: his girlfriend, Gemma, his partner, Carlo, and that car. The thought of two of them being shot at simultaneously made his stomach turn.

"I want my fucking eye back, asshole!" Ling shouted during a pause in the endless barrage of gunfire.

The Chinese gang leader wasn't much to look at. Barely five feet tall and a shade over one hundred pounds, Ling made up for his shortcomings with a ruthlessness befitting a wild dog. He was mean, sure, but so trumped-up that he invited challengers, peacocking around in suede suits and alligator-skin shoes. His Magic 8 Ball glass eye turned him into a cruel joke, a comic book villain committing real-world crimes.

The kind of guy who had matching gold-plated Berettas.

But while Ling himself might have been a joke, his money and guns were not. Seb needed more than one hand to count the weapons aimed his way.

Still, Seb hadn't started the day thinking he'd screw over the nefarious drug lord. In fact, he just wanted to fence some diamonds and other jewelry he and Carlo had stolen from a pawnshop in Reno. Ling, a man of many criminal undertakings, had promised them a fair price on the stash, but when it came time to make the deal—two o'clock in that department store parking lot—Ling had the audacity to show up with an empty wallet.

EIGHT CYLINDERS

But Ling wasn't empty-handed. Instead, he'd brought along several kilos of cocaine to barter with. Both Seb and Carlo had their fair share of vices—drinking, gambling, armed robbery, extortion, and the occasional traffic violation—but neither was prone to dancing with Lady Snow. Further compounding the situation, neither Seb nor Carlo understood the metric system. In short, the cocaine was worthless to them.

Seeing the deal going south faster than a robin in winter, Seb had grabbed Ling to use as a human shield and backed away. Just for fun, he'd plucked out the glass eye.

Seven of Ling's men stared and growled threats, but it was Ling who'd freed himself with a kick of his heel up between Seb's legs. He and Carlo had been very lucky to make it behind the Impala before the shooting began.

A tire on the other side of the Impala blew out with a pop and a long hiss. Carlo nudged him with his foot. "Will you put that away and help me think of a way out of here?"

Seb rolled the polished glass eye between his fingers, smudging it. "Why don't we ask the Magic 8 Ball?"

"I'm not sure you should be touching that. It just seems so . . . unsanitary."

Seb shrugged. "All right, then. Here's the plan. On the count of three, I'm going to throw this back to Ling. As soon as I let go, we run."

Carlo frowned and turned his nose up in obvious disgust. "That's your genius plan?"

Seb cocked his head at his partner's sudden somberness. Carlo had always been the carefree one,

3

the man with the easy smile that made easy women swoon. Things always worked out for Carlo. To see his friend concerned, even if only a little, Seb had to wonder if he'd finally gotten them into trouble he couldn't get them out of.

"You've got a better idea?"

Carlo sighed. "Guess not. Well, it's been real."

Seb laughed. "That it has." He shook his friend's hand. Outwardly, the two couldn't have been more different. Carlo looked like a centerfold for Hitler's male review, while Seb was only a shade lighter than obsidian. Their differences were only skin-deep. They were of the same mind on nearly everything. Sharing many a job, a residence, and once, even a woman, the two were closer than conjoined twins.

Their levity fell off them like shed skin. "On three," Seb said, "run for the car."

"You don't need to tell me twice." Carlo's easy smile returned.

Somehow, that worried Seb more. He prodded some loose pavement with his foot. A section the size of his fist came free. He shook the 8 Ball and whispered, "Is this going to work?"

Better not tell you now.

Seb frowned and jabbed the novelty glass eye into his pocket, picking up the larger, heavier chunk of cement to throw at Ling. The Charger was parked no more than ten spaces away and, so far, out of the line of fire. Its shiny chrome rims beckoned him. If they could just make it inside the car, he was confident he could get them out of there.

Seb threw up a finger. "One."

Carlo threw up two.

"Hey, Ling!" Seb raised a hand then drew his arm back. "You want your eye back? Catch!"

The chunk of pavement sailed through the air as both Carlo and Seb shouted, "Three!" A window on one of Ling's vehicles shattered, immediately followed by a slew of Chinese curse words. Carlo and Seb stood and started blasting. Neither turned to run.

"What are you waiting for?" Seb shouted over the gunfire. "I'll cover you."

"You go," Carlo answered. "I'll cover you."

Their bullets had temporarily alleviated the counter spray in their direction, but it was only a matter of time before Ling's men rediscovered their balls. The two thieves had no time to argue.

Seb nodded. "Fine. I'll get the car. Stay here and stay low."

"Give my regards to Gemma," Carlo said, clicking his teeth and flashing that sometimes infuriatingly carefree smile. He only took his eyes off the enemy for a second. In the next second, he was dropping to the cement, half his brain splattered against the pavement.

"Carlo!" The sight of his friend falling sent Seb into a fury. He stood up straight, planted his arms on the Impala's hood, took aim, and fired until his clip was empty. When he had finished, he'd reduced Ling's team by at least two men.

Click, click, click.

Reason and fear returned, and he dropped back behind the car to reload. Carlo's cold dead eyes stared blankly at him. Seb saw no accusation, no call for justice. Just a reflection of himself and the fate that awaited him if he didn't get moving.

His mouth fell open in a silent scream. An ache

burned deep in his chest as he fought back tears. The 8 Ball seemed to vibrate in his pocket, and without thinking, he reached for it. Giving it a shake, he asked, "Can I kill them all?"

My sources say no.

"I'll kill them for you, Carlo." He clenched his jaw. "Maybe not today, but someday."

As he lay down atop his fallen friend, he saw a pair of feet approaching the front of the Impala. He had to assume another pair was approaching the rear. Ling's men were trying to flank him.

He ripped a new clip from his pocket while the spent one slid out. After jamming in the fresh clip, he pulled back the hammer and turned to shoot at the man who was circling the front of the car.

Seb fired one shot, a good one that took the man in the neck just as he came into view. He swung around and fired at the man approaching from the rear. Seb popped him in the chest then in the stomach, and the man fell.

Though he'd only fired twice at the second guy, he could have sworn he'd heard three gunshots. That was when his side exploded in pain.

His white button-down blossomed with a dark red swell, rapidly expanding from a point about four inches above his waist. He cringed, his head lolling back, his eyes rolling in their sockets, as he tried to breathe through the pain.

"He's been hit," Ling said. "Get him."

Ling's crew had taken some losses, but by Seb's count, he was still outgunned four to one. Five, if he counted both of Ling's Berettas. Tears blurred his vision. He needed to move if he ever hoped to avenge Carlo or see his beautiful Gemma again.

EIGHT CYLINDERS

He crawled under the Jeep and shuffled along the cement to the other side. Once there, he would need to sprint about twenty yards to his Charger with its seven hundred seven horsepower, six-point-two-liter Hemi V-8 engine, and six-hundred-fifty-pound-feet of torque. It could go from zero to sixty in a matter of seconds, less time than it would take him to reach the damn thing.

He was vaguely aware that he was trailing blood. Every time he pulled himself forward, his wound felt as if it were tearing open a little more. Sweat poured from his forehead and dampened his armpits. Blood lubed up his jeans.

If he wanted to live, he needed to move. Seb wanted to live. On the other side of the Jeep, he remote-started the Charger and pushed himself to his feet, his legs slow and shaky at first as they tried to propel him forward. They firmed up when he heard one of Ling's enforcers shout, "There he is!" He made it to his passenger-side door before the first shot whipped by. The door was unlocked. He yanked it open then scrambled over to the driver's seat, jerked the car into drive, and punched the gas. Tires burned as they spun over the pavement.

Under a heavy rain of bullets, Seb sped out of the lot. He lost sight of Ling's men before they could hop into their vehicles and follow.

He pulled the car onto the freeway, knowing only that he wanted out of that commercial district, away from the casino lights and endless traffic. He was vaguely aware he was driving out of the city, away from Gemma, away from his dead partner and the life he had known, away from any hospital he knew—or any help. His panicked, fogged-up thinking screamed that he needed to get out.

Bent into claws from constant straining, his fingers wouldn't obey his mind's command to slacken. He'd been driving one-handed. The other hand had been squeezing the glass eye as if it were trying to form a diamond from a lump of coal.

Tears came then, with the realization that he might die, that Gemma and Carlo were lost to him, and he lost to the world. He shook the ball. "Am I going to die?"

Yes.

He smacked a bloodied palm against his forehead. "Stupid question. Everyone dies." He shook the ball again. "Am I going to die soon?"

Cannot predict now.

"Fuck!" He rolled down his window. "Useless piece of shit!" He cocked back his arm to toss the 8 Ball into oncoming traffic.

Instead, he shook it again. "Which way do I go if I want to live?"

Reply hazy try again.

Seb laughed, delirious then, his vision blurring. The streetlights looked like tractor beams from UFOs. The dotted lines whipped by so fast they appeared solid.

In his fogged-up, fucked-up state, exhausted and cold, so cold, he landed on the idea that, somehow, that cursed eyeball was guiding him. A saner voice, one that might have been louder in his normal, blood-filled mind, questioned the reason behind that conclusion, but it was killed off by an angst and fear-driven compulsion to find a way to live.

EIGHT CYLINDERS

The 8 Ball was his ticket. Seb just needed to ask the right questions.

Yes or no questions.

"Should I take the next exit?" He shook the ball.

Yes definitely.

"Should I take a left off the exit?"

My reply is no.

"Turn here?"

Yes.

"Head straight?"

Yes definitely.

And so Seb drove and continued to drive, leaving his course in the hands of a gangster's novelty toy, never questioning the logic of it all. His eyelids began to flutter. It became harder and harder to keep the car on the road. Until he was no longer on the road at all.

Still, he drove on, out into nowhere, mountains, deserts, and barely traveled dirt paths his only hope for salvation.

"Where am I?" he muttered.

His car began to slow. As he rolled forward, he asked the 8 Ball, "Did you bring me out here to die?"

Without a doubt.

He laughed between sobs and shook it again, the hopeless act of a man who had followed a false prophet into oblivion. "Why?"

Concentrate and ask again. The words almost seemed to mock him.

He rested his head against the steering wheel, so weak now, still chuckling, still crying, all hope slipping away with the steady stream of his blood. *Is this it? Is this the end?* He fell limp against the wheel, the 8 Ball tumbling from his hand. It rolled along the carpet at

his feet then stopped, the window to its bubbly interior facing up.
 Ask again later.

CHAPTER 2

A SOFT TAPPING on Seb's cheek woke him from anxious dreams that vanished with the light, his thudding heart and a short gasp the last indicators of a fretful slumber. A long pink tongue lolled over his face, and hot breath blew through his eyebrows. Another droplet of drool spattered on the bridge of his nose.

Fangs? Seb stared, bewildered, at the saliva-gleaming teeth set in black gums then pushed the short-haired mutt away. Getting a closer look at the animal, he gasped, jerked back in his bed, and cowered against the wall. He sputtered, struggling to speak, until words came to him at last. "A fucking coyote!"

Fear snapped away whatever fogginess remained. Seb groaned in pain, his side burning from the sudden movement. Bandages were wrapped so tightly around his otherwise bare ribs that he could hardly breathe. The room he found himself in was so swelteringly hot that his bandages were wet from a combination of blood and sweat. The bedsheets around him, not his own, were likewise soaked. On top of them, more disturbing than the foreign surroundings, was a coyote, standing sentinel.

A fat man in overalls entered the room, holding a glass of water and carrying with him an aroma of bacon grease and unwashed gym socks. He walked up beside the canine and stroked it behind the ear.

"This here's Juke," the man said, patting the coyote's side. "He's a big softie." He snapped his fingers, and Juke jumped off the bed to sit on his haunches at his master's feet.

"And I'm Earl," the man continued. "I guess you can say I'm what passes for a doctor in these parts." His triceps hung loose, jiggling as he extended his arms, offering the water to Seb. His extra weight hid some of the lines in his face but not enough to conceal the marks of someone tired and worn. Sweat ran in a V down his stained white T-shirt and beaded on his forehead, beneath close-cropped blond hair.

"I'm also the village mechanic, cook, handyman... you name it. Round here, we all wear a lot of hats. Those of us that are left, anyway." He laughed. "Man, have we got a lot of questions for you."

Seb crept forward on the bed, his eyes trained on the strange pet. His side screamed with pain as he reached for the water. With the stinging came recollection. He'd been shot. Carlo, his partner, took one in the head. *Did he make it to the car? No, he was already dead. Where's the car? Fucking Ling.* He scowled. Ling's men had all but chased him out of Vegas. *That was... how long ago was that?*

And how did I get here? He looked around for his gun, but it, his clothes, his things—all were missing. He was naked. His face flushed, and he pulled the sheet over himself. He couldn't remember the last time he'd been without his piece, and he didn't like the feeling. For that matter, he couldn't remember the last time he woke up naked in a stranger's home, and the coyote was a whole new element entirely. He laughed uneasily. *Gemma will not approve.*

"Where's my, uh, shirt?" he asked after thanking Earl and handing him the empty glass. He swallowed hard. Had Ling's men caught him? The big man didn't look like any of Ling's enforcers. First, he wasn't Chinese. Second, most of Ling's brutes didn't use their barrel guts to hold up overalls, the shoulder loops hanging around their knees. Third, Seb wasn't bound.

That begged the question, "Where am I?"

"Someplace safe, relatively speaking, and out of danger. You were hurt bad, son. Sorry we don't have no painkillers we could give you." Earl shrugged. "Anyhow, your stuff is in the drawer over there." He pointed at a dresser against the far wall. "We washed your clothes as best we could, but some stains just won't be scrubbed out. Your gun's over there. Your phone, too, but I don't think either of them will do you a whole lot of good here."

"Where's here, exactly?"

"That's a difficult question to answer, son, on account of the fact that this here town ain't got no name." He raised his palms apologetically. "Ain't much of a town, neither. More like an outpost. Back in the army, we might have called it a FOB."

Seb had never been in the army and wasn't familiar with the term, but he didn't care enough to ask for an explanation. He ran a hand over his bandages. They were clean and dry. "The army? That where you learned to patch me up?"

"Yessir." Earl nodded and stroked the coyote. "Got

that bullet out clean, too. Sewed you up real nice. You're welcome."

"Thank you . . . but I don't get it. Last thing I remember, I was burning rubber out of Vegas, bleeding out all over my seat." *Was something giving me directions?* "Next thing I know, I'm waking up here."

Earl frowned. "You don't remember much, huh? We were hoping you could tell us how you got through the pass, but I'm not surprised. You lost a lot of blood. And I mean *a lot* of blood. You're lucky Juke found you and came and got me when he did."

"Uh . . . thanks, boy." His hand shaking slightly, Seb reached out and scratched Juke under the chin. The coyote squinted and leaned into him. Seb relaxed.

Earl tapped his chin. "You must have gotten yourself into some serious shit back in Sin City, winding up here in the state you did."

Seb opened his mouth to speak, not knowing what kind of lie he would have to spin, but Earl threw up his hand. "No need to explain. Ain't no one here who hasn't done things he or she ain't proud of."

Seb smiled. "Does it make a difference if I only did mine to people who deserved it?"

"Don't rightly know if it's my place to say, son."

Seb decided he liked his savior. He extended his hand. "Sebastian McCalister. Friends call me Seb."

Earl shook his hand. "Earl Crenshaw. People 'round here call me Doc, but I prefer my God-given name."

"You keep coyotes as pets *'round here*?" Seb asked, trying out the phrase.

"Believe you me, they ain't got nowhere else to be.

But we lost Fanny last week. Or two weeks ago maybe. She was this one's mate. Juke here's the only one left now, only one smart enough to stay put." Earl petted the animal softly. "I think he kinda took her loss hard."

"How'd she die?" Seb asked, not much caring but thinking he should ask.

"Same as everyone else 'round here does eventually, I suppose."

Seb squinted up at Earl, the answer having spurred his curiosity. But the big man apparently felt no need to elaborate.

"You hungry?" Earl crossed his arms and rested them on his belly. "I imagine you would be."

Seb's stomach growled in answer. He was more than hungry; he was outright starving. "How long was I out?"

"You arrived the night before last. We found you yesterday morning, asleep at the wheel, parked beside this here shack, which, to your good fortune, just became vacant last . . . month? A few months ago? Whenever." He slapped his thighs. "We're surprised no one heard you come in, though. At night, it's so deathly quiet 'round here, you'd swear the whole world had come to an end. Even the mountains are . . . well, never you mind that now. Get dressed, and I'll fix you up some lunch, introduce you to the others."

Earl turned to leave, but he stopped at the door. "I hope you ain't a picky eater." He stared at the wall over Seb, lost somewhere deep in thought. "On second thought, maybe you should bring your gun." He left with Juke pattering at his heels.

Seb winced as he got out of bed. Every part of him ached, as though he'd gone twelve rounds as a human punching bag. Checking himself for injuries, he found only the one wound, but the one was bad enough. The bullet had missed his heart for sure, hence the fact that he was still alive. It had entered his body between his lower two ribs and somehow managed not to completely shatter either of them. At least, nothing felt broken. How the bullet hadn't struck some other vital organ—his lung or his liver or some shit—was a miracle unto itself.

Although his body objected to his every movement, the dull protests of bruised and torn muscles were all that accompanied its complaints. He supposed he'd been hit by a ricochet or the bullet had gone through something—*or someone? Carlo?*—before hitting him, wounding him only skin-deep. But if that were so, why had he lost so much blood?

No, he had been lying down. It was all coming back then. Ling's enforcer had gotten off a clean shot. He was damn lucky to be alive.

No thanks to that fucking eye. The thought came unbidden, and it took him a second to understand it. *Did I really let that stupid thing decide my fate? I'm such an asshole.* He flexed his fingers, smoothed down his bandages, and felt all the agony of the living, paired with the flushed-face humiliation of having to acknowledge that a stupid fortune-telling glass eye had led him out into nowhere. That eye had somehow gifted him life.

He shook his head. *You're no freaking doctor, Sebastian. You could be dying where you stand.* Not trusting the thoroughness of some redneck combat medic he'd just met, he figured he'd need to see a real doctor as soon as he got out of there, wherever *there* was. And he would use Google Maps or Waze to lead him, not some silly toy.

For the first time, he took in his surroundings. His bed was barely more than a bunk, a wet spot in the shape of his body staining where he'd lain. His skin glistened with sweat, the water he'd drunk pouring itself right back out of him. The air itself seemed a mixture of moisture and musk.

The walls of his one-room hut were thin plywood, hastily crafted, with one window, the kind that opened up and outward by turning a small crank. The roof was comprised of ridged metal sheets that glowed red beneath the hot sun, baking the room beneath it. Fine sand spackled an earthen floor. A small battery-operated fan atop a dresser circulated the fiery air but did nothing to cool it.

Other than the bunk and the dresser, the room had few accoutrements. A sink was attached to the wall near one corner, where a disconnected toilet lay tipped over on its side. As if sensing Seb's eyes upon it, a scorpion with little opaque babies on its back scrambled under the bowl. Above the sink hung a grimy mirror.

Seb's thirst unsatisfied, he hurried to the sink and put his mouth under the faucet. When he turned the knob, the pipes groaned and clanked, but no water came out. As he waited, willing cool liquid to come while the plumbing continued to bellow, a long-legged centipede tiptoed soundlessly from the spigot, no doubt annoyed by the disturbance echoing through its home.

With his palm, Seb wiped the grime from the mirror and gasped. He almost didn't recognize the man he saw. Only twenty-eight years old, Seb was still young and healthy, but his reflection looked at least ten years older and paler than any proud black man ever wanted to be. A laugh burst from his cracked lips, its sudden emergence snapping him out of despair. His reflection was a stranger to him.

Stranger still was the man who stood behind him. Half his head was missing, but Seb recognized the black leather jacket with straps hanging from the cuffs and the easy smile plastered across his face. His smile vanished. Seb froze. "Carlo?" He stared at the reflection of his longtime running mate. Carlo stared back at him, his eyes milky and glossy. He reached for Seb. His heart leaping in his throat, Seb dove for the dresser. In a flash, he snatched up his gun and twirled around to face . . .

No one. Seb blinked and studied the room. He was alone unless he counted the bugs. *Get a hold of yourself. You're losing it.*

No, his mind was sound. Blood loss had caused him to hallucinate. That was all. *Some food will do you good.*

But first, call Gemma. She'll be freaking out by now. Seb played it cool as he reached for his phone, but in truth, he wanted little more than to hear Gemma's voice and know she was safe. He'd been out too long, long enough for Ling to pay their apartment a visit, looking for him. Gemma was smart and knew how to handle herself, two of the many qualities he loved about her. But he hadn't even been able to warn her that the Ling deal had gone poorly, that Carlo was dead. When he never came home, she must have suspected the worst.

Why didn't I just go home? Why didn't I call her? He shook his head as he examined the blank black screen of his cell phone. *Why the hell did I come here? 'Cause Ling's eye told me to?* He smacked his palm against his forehead. *Stupid. She's gonna have my balls in a jar for a month.*

Seb pressed the power button and the phone turned on, but waves ran over the screen as if it were a TV receiving a scrambled signal. He tapped his finger against one app then another, tried to get access to his touchpad and, when that failed, his email, all with no success. Perhaps he had damaged it in all the excitement.

He tossed the phone aside and struggled to dress. In addition to the agony of movement, his clothes clung to him as he tried to pull them on. Once dressed, he checked the safety on his gun then tucked it into his waistband, pulling the tails of his button-down over it. He checked his pockets for . . . *for what?* He chuckled. *That fucker's eye.* His laughter quickly faded. Whether the 8 Ball had helped him out of there or not, it had left Carlo behind. *So fuck that piece of shit.*

His chin shook, so he let the anger in. After wiping the sweat from his brow with his sleeve, he rolled it and its pair up to his elbows and headed for the door.

Then he stepped out into the blinding sunlight.

The air was so hot that it singed Seb's throat as he sucked it in. The coarse black hairs on his arms and head sucked up so much sun they felt like hot plates against his skin. When his eyes at last adjusted, he found himself surrounded by sand and dust. To his left, to his right, and under his feet, a flat expanse of desert spread out to the horizon. There, mountains rose like sharp gray teeth biting at the sky. They seemed miles away, jagged, snowless caps as hard and unwelcoming as the empty oblivion between. He imagined they were the mountains he'd flown over so many times coming to and from McCarran Airport. Not once in all those flights, in spite of their proximity to home, had Seb ever been inclined to visit those dreary ranges. Many of the worst sins of Las Vegas were deposited there, countless bodies buried deep but not always deep enough: shallow graves dug up by animals, skeletal bones scattered, exposed, and bleached white by the sun.

Burned clean.

Directly in front of him, a tent large enough to cover a one-ring circus stood still as a frozen lake, except for a sporadic rustle in a breeze. Seb wished he could feel. From inside came the sounds of voices too low to understand.

Beyond the tent, more mountains loomed. They seemed to border the entire enclave. He turned around but could see only his shack and another to the left.

Seb ran around the corner of the ragtag structure and nearly collided with the ass end of his Dodge Charger. It was parked neatly alongside the shack. The car was the closest thing he had to a pet, and it was in desperate need of a wash. Just seeing its satin-black spoiler and performance tires made him crave the open road. Though he loved both Carlo and Gemma more than the ride, both had seemed jealous of the attention he poured into it.

Carlo. Seb smiled over his pain. His partner's face, with its bullet hole leaking blood, flashed in the Charger's rear window and vanished as quickly as it had come. Seb's pulse quickened. He rubbed his eyes with his palms. *Get ahold of yourself,* he chided himself more firmly. He ran his fingers through his hair. *Get a fucking grip, man.*

Seb circled the car to the driver's side door. His fingers glided along the frame. The heat of the metal made him wince, then smile to find something familiar in that unfamiliar place, and he smiled wider when he found the keys still in the ignition. He dove in through the open window, pulled them out, and shoved them into his pocket.

He scanned the distance behind the shack. Five or six more structures like his—small, hastily constructed, termite-riddled boxes with tin-can roofs—were positioned around a dusty well. Aside from them and the large tent that seemed to have even less business being out there than the shacks themselves, Seb saw nothing but desert.

And more freakin' mountains. He spun around. The mountains circled that desolate place, the small population dead center, like a pupil in a giant yellow eye. The way they walled in that flat land made his throat tighten. Though he couldn't explain why, he felt trapped.

Shielding his eyes with his hands, Seb scanned the mountains, looking for a pass. For a moment, he thought one of the peaks had moved, but the heat waves rising off the baking clay ground made everything at a distance blur and shimmer. Still, his unease at looking at that dark, silent range bordered on dread.

"Where the fuck are you, Sebastian, and how the fuck did you end up here?" Wanting answers, he turned and headed toward the tent.

CHAPTER 3

INSIDE THE TENT, the air hung heavy and wet. Within moments, his clothes were heavier. The rank smells of stale sweat and unwashed armpits carried on moisture so thick, he thought he could taste them.

The high-ceilinged tent at least offered some escape from the blazing sun. He hadn't realized how hot and red his skin had become in such a short time. It must have been well over a hundred degrees outside. He'd heard Death Valley sometimes hit temperatures as high as one thirty. Was that where he'd driven?

He pulled the front of his shirt away from his chest. The temperature inside wasn't much better. He rolled his eyes. *It's not the heat but the humidity.*

"Sebastian," Earl bellowed from the end of a long table. "Come meet the rest of the group."

A cluster of some of the poorest, mangiest excuses for the human condition huddled around the table. They sat on milk crates and stacks of cardboard—six adults, all of whom appeared to be male, and one child, an Asian girl who looked about twelve years old. The table itself sat in the middle of a rectangle of more dead earth.

"Hurry up, boss," said a barrel of a man with a

mullet and a long scar down the side of his face. "We're hungry." Sleeve tattoos, faded green with age and exposure, covered his arms. Their cousins sprouted from his T-shirt collar. The bar code under his chin identified him as a member of the Boss Hogs, a biker gang out of Reno. Seb's dealings with them had always been straightforward and fair. He found the presence of another nod to life outside that god-awful place comforting.

But any comfort Seb had felt vanished when he took in the train wreck who sat next to Bar Code, a twitchy, pale-skinned, sweaty, nervous-looking skeleton of a man, with pubescent scruff growing in patches on his cheeks and darting eyes that looked both cruel and desperate. His fingers rolled over the grip of a pistol. With his other hand, he scratched at his elbow. His flippant grin was full of black gaps between black teeth. The man had *junkie* written all over him, and Seb didn't doubt the tweaker would do anything for another fix or even a chance at one. Somehow, he doubted any of the local shacks contained a meth lab.

Unless . . . he considered the remoteness and the emptiness of the place. The Boss Hogs were known drug traffickers, sometimes riding the hurricane highway straight from Mexico. Maybe he'd landed himself in some cartel way station, a pit stop between Mexico and L.A. That thought made Seb's skin prickle. What would that mean for his chances of getting out?

Relax, man. If they wanted you dead, you'd be dead already.

"I want to know how he got here," said an old woman with a shaved head, whom Seb had first mistaken for a man. She wore a long fishhook as an earring and had skin as hard and wrinkled as leather. When she turned toward Seb, he could see her right eye was missing. He couldn't help but think that she and Ling had at least one thing in common.

"We all got questions," said a young man wearing a baseball cap. He didn't look any older than twenty. The front of his hat featured the silhouette of a naked woman. The figure's hands, though ambiguous, seemed to each disappear into an orifice. "But I am hungry, man. Can't wait no more, Doc." He grinned, baring teeth stained yellow.

Another crackhead, Seb thought, *but at least this one still has most of his teeth*. His mind again turned over the idea that he'd landed in some sort of drug highway, surrounded by cartel mules.

A large black man with fists the size of sledgehammers pounded the table, silencing the room. He stared at Seb with fierce bloodshot eyes. Seb was no small man himself and, having sized up most of the room already, thought he could hold his own against any one or two of the people there. All except Sledgehammer Fists. Mr. Fists could probably outwrestle a bear. If things in that strange place turned sour, Seb knew whose side he hoped to be on.

"Thanks, Malcolm," Earl said from the head of the table. He pointed at each person present, starting with Bar Code, then at Junkie Number One. "Sebastian, meet Red and Sly." He waved his hand over to the other side. "That's Helen, Skeeter, and Malcolm." He pointed at the old woman, the young man in the cap, and Sledgehammer Fists, respectively.

The large man grunted and nodded.

EIGHT CYLINDERS

Earl chuckled. "Malcolm here is the strong, silent type."

He then swung his arm to his right, where a little Asian girl sat beside him. Her skin was a patchwork of reds and purples, scar tissue from second- and third-degree burns. The big man's arm brushed against her, and she screamed then curled into a ball.

"I'm sorry, Mary." Earl fumbled. "I . . . I didn't mean to." He sighed and looked up at Seb. "This here's Mary. She doesn't say much either. And as you might have guessed, she doesn't like to be touched."

Red laughed. "Another way she's kind of like you, huh, Malcolm?"

Earl ignored him. "Everyone, meet Sebastian."

"Hi, how ya doing, and all that bullshit," Helen said.

"Nice to meet you." Seb nodded. "Say, um, I don't suppose anyone's got a phone I can borrow real quick? Mine's busted."

"They're all busted out here, son," Earl added. "We can't get any messages in or out, not by phone, not by email . . . not even by the damn Pony Express. Cell phones are good for about one thing: paperweights."

"They still vibrate," Helen added.

Skeeter laughed. Red shook his head. "That's disgusting."

Helen faked innocence. "What?"

Seb would not be derailed. "But Vegas must have a thousand cell towers. We can't be that far—"

"They don't work," Skeeter said, his tone irritable. "Can we eat now?"

As if on cue, a Latina in her mid-thirties entered through a flap in the side of the tent. A partition separated the adjacent room from the remainder of the tent. Seb couldn't see what was on the other side of the wall, but at that moment, he didn't care to look. The woman was a beauty, with sun-darkened skin and dark features. She wore a buttoned shirt tied in the front and light tan capris. Over her shoulder, she carried a tray with eight paper plates on it.

Seb's mouth watered, his attention shifting from the woman to what she carried. He took a seat beside Red, his eyes never leaving the tray in the woman's hand. The smell of roasted meat masked the stench of those who would be eating it, and his stomach ached for a savory, salty steak.

Sly rubbed his hands together as the woman held the tray in the middle of the table. He slapped her ass as she leaned over to put it down.

The woman froze, balancing the tray over the table in a precarious way that must have required both tremendous strength and balance. The glare she shot Sly bordered on a snarl.

This woman has teeth, Seb thought, the ferocity bringing the hint of a smile to his face, a reminder of the firecracker he had waiting for him back home.

She growled, yelled something in Spanish, and looked as though she would break Sly's remaining teeth by jamming the tray down his throat. She dropped the tray with a thud into the center of the greedy horde. Everyone lunged for a plate, including Mary and Seb. When he pulled the plate in front of him, Seb salivated momentarily over the half of the meal that sizzled.

The other half moved.

Seb snapped up straight and pulled back his hands.

While the others hungrily dug in, tearing apart flesh and scooping up squirming mouthfuls with their fingers, Seb paused to reconsider, disgust overtaking his hunger.

On one side of his plate, sizzling meat lay in a pool of grease. It smelled delicious, like ribs hot out of a smoker. But beside it, mealworms wriggled and made porous what looked like stale and blackened bread.

Despite his stomach turning, he picked up the meat and took a bite. To his delight, it tasted good, almost like some kind of jerked pork or spicy sausage. Until it crunched. He pulled the meat out of his mouth. Rows of tiny bones lined it.

He looked at Earl. "What is this?"

"Snake," Earl replied with his mouth full. "Not half bad, is it? And them there on your plate are grubs. We used to cook 'em right outside in the sun on a sheet of metal. It helped with the texture and, uh, the movement, but they'd stick to the pan and, frankly, lose all their flavor." He shoveled a handful of squirming critters into his mouth as easily as Seb would wolf down Tater Tots. "As you might imagine, we don't have a lot to eat around here. Grubs are high in protein and will give you the strength to endure this . . . this place." He shrugged. "We had to eat worse in the army."

Seb pushed his plate away from him. "I don't plan on enduring it here any longer than I need to."

The others froze.

Seb made no attempt to pull back his plate.

Earl hefted a breath. His shoulders drooped. "Look, son, I know it ain't exactly Nobu or whatever you're used to in Vegas, but it'll keep you alive. Heck, despite as little as I've eaten and all the sweating I do, I don't think I've even lost a pound since I got here."

After a moment of silence, Sly made his move. The others followed suit, each snatching what they could of Seb's meal, except for Mary, who stole a few grubs from Earl's plate while he was distracted.

Her eyes locked with Seb's, filling with awareness that he'd caught her. She slammed the grubs into her mouth and swallowed, smirking as if to say, "Too late."

All ate noisily except the woman who had brought them the food. She fixed her cold brown eyes on Seb. He couldn't help but stare back, trying to guess at the reason for such blatant hostility.

Red nudged him, shaking his gaze away from hers. "She eats in back while preparing it. Sly thinks maybe it's so she can sneak extra." He pointed at Juke who appeared by the woman's side as if out of thin air. "With that mongrel."

Seb didn't respond but re-engaged the younger woman in a staring contest. She produced a large bone from perhaps the same place Juke had been hiding. Its origin, both in respect to what it had once been part of and where it had most recently been hiding, was a mystery. Seb thought it could be human. Wherever and whatever it had come from, the coyote snatched it up greedily.

After most of them had finished, having averted his eyes from the feast as much as possible, he asked, "What is this place? Why do you all live like this?"

"You don't get to ask the questions, newbie." Helen's face contorted into a mask of hate and condemnation. "We've been waiting almost two days for your sorry ass to wake up."

"Come now, Helen," Earl said. "Be nice to our guest." He leveled his gaze on Seb. "But tell me again, for the benefit of the others, where you came from and how you got here. And spare no details. Ain't none of us here innocent, 'cept Mary here."

Seb took a deep breath. He recounted the tale of how he'd seen his best friend and partner gunned down by an angry mobster and himself fleeing for his life, how he was shot in the process and had burned rubber straight the hell out of Sin City. He left out the part where he had followed a Magic 8 Ball eyeball on some delirium-induced vision quest and neglected to mention the girlfriend waiting for him back in Vegas, one whom Ling would surely leverage to get to him.

He clenched his teeth. *Gemma's tough as nails. She can take care of herself.* While every part of him knew that to be true, his practical side saw it as a simple numbers game. She was one against an army. And he had not only caused that fate but also had abandoned her to it.

He wrapped up his tale and determined to leave as soon as possible. "And when I woke up, I was here." Seb lifted his shirt to show his bandages. "I guess I've got your Doc to thank that I even woke up at all."

Everyone stared at him in silence.

Until Sly broke it. "No. No, man. You have to remember something."

Red grunted. "Yeah, cut the bullshit. How'd you get through the mountains?"

"I must have just driven here, I guess." Seb shrugged. "Honestly, I don't remember how I even got off the highway. Earl says I lost a lot of blood."

Earl nodded. "That's putting it mildly, son."

Sly scoffed. "You just drove here? This nig—"

Malcolm jumped to his feet, his fists and teeth clenched. The death stare he gave Sly made the lanky man shrivel.

Skeeter picked up where Sly faltered. "Sly's right, guys. This dude's pulling our dicks. No one just drives here."

Helen's eyes brightened. "Maybe he came at just the right time. Maybe they sleep—"

"Horseshit." Red slapped his hand against the table. "We *know* they don't sleep."

"Well, he's here, and before that, he wasn't." Earl's words were like lapping waves, soothing in their ebb and flow. "More than that, his car's here."

Skeeter straightened. "Maybe he hang glided or parachuted in."

"With his car?" Earl chuckled. "That must have been a sight. And what happened to the chute?"

Skeeter paused, opened his mouth to say something else, then shut it. He sighed.

The Hispanic woman said something in her native tongue.

Seb frowned. He didn't speak Spanish.

Earl must have noticed his confusion. "Angelique says it could be in your trunk."

"Nah," Helen said. She shrank back into her chair. "I already checked that for anything we could use."

Seb squinted her way, and she avoided eye contact. He guessed he couldn't blame her or any of them for distrusting him, a stranger appearing in the middle of the night and looking like death itself.

"Is it really that surprising?" Earl showed his palms. "Do any of us really remember—"

"No, no, no, no, *no!*" Sly stood up, a tick causing his eye to twitch. "This fucker knows something! He found a way through the mountains. Shit, maybe he just got lucky. Or maybe they're gone." He pulled a gun from his waistband. "Or maybe he's the reason we're stuck here in the first place!"

Seb's hand crept toward his pistol, but Earl threw out a steadying hand. "Now, Sly, we need to all just calm down."

"Fuck that, Doc." Sly jerked his arm at Seb. "I say we torture the fucker until he tells us everything he knows." A smile curled the corners of his mouth, as if the idea of torture appealed to him and he was trying to conceal it.

Malcolm rose again. "Put your gun away before I shove it up your psychotic ass."

"Psychotic?" Sly smirked. "You don't think I know you? What you did? It was all over the news, asshole. How many people did you gun down? Sixteen? Seventeen?"

Malcolm's eyes watered. "That was . . . I didn't mean . . . " He sat down and covered his face with his hands.

Sly laughed. "Yeah, that's what I thought." He stepped toward Seb and jerked the pistol at his face. "Now, you'd better start talking or—"

Seb grabbed Sly's wrist and twisted, snatching the gun with his other hand. He pressed it under Sly's chin. "Never point a gun at me again." He pushed Sly away.

His face reddening, Sly sat down. He rubbed his wrist.

"Everyone listen," Seb began, "'cause I'm only

going to say this once. I don't know what kind of fucked-up party y'all are throwing here, and I don't want to. The only reason I've stayed this long was 'cause I was hoping to catch some halfway-decent grub." His stomach gurgled, and he swallowed the bit of its contents that had risen at his poor choice of words. He raised Sly's gun and drew his own, swinging both at the crowd.

"Now, if you don't mind, I'll be taking my leave. Anyone moves, and the rest of you will have a new kind of fresh meat to try." He backed toward the opening at the front of the tent.

"I wouldn't do that," Earl said.

Helen gasped. "He really doesn't know, does he?"

Sly grimaced. "Fuck him. He wouldn't believe us if we told him, anyway."

Seb didn't know what kind of game they were playing, but he'd reached the limit of his patience. His back hit the tent flap. He could feel hot sun on his legs. It was high time he got the hell out of Dodge.

In a Dodge Charger.

"You'll die if you try to leave," Earl said flatly.

Seb frowned. "Oh yeah? Is that a threat?"

"Just a fact, son. Stay awhile. Let me explain."

But Seb was done listening. "Adios." He backed out of the tent and tucked Sly's gun into his left pocket. As he sprinted for his car, he pulled his keys from his right pocket. He yanked open the metal latch, singeing his fingers as he did. Jumping on the black leather seats, he choked back a yelp, thankful he hadn't been wearing shorts. He turned the key, rolled up the windows, and jacked up the AC, then said a little prayer before grabbing the black steering wheel.

His wheels spun in the sand as he popped the car into gear and slammed down the pedal. He fishtailed as he one-eightied, figuring the way out had to be in the opposite direction.

When the dust settled behind him, he saw the biker and the old woman watching him go. He raised his middle finger. "See ya."

An engine roared, and two vehicles spun into view behind him. "You've gotta be kidding me." The beat-up pickup, driven by Skeeter—he knew because he could make out the ball cap—caused him no concern. He couldn't tell what make it was, only that it had seen better days, holes rusted straight through its metal bits, paint faded where it wasn't peeling. The whole vehicle rattled as it moved. It would never catch him.

The Humvee with a mounted turret was another matter.

"What in the hell . . . " Seb was speechless. The vehicle behind him belonged in Desert Storm not Desert Outside Vegas. The Humvee was big and armored and was tearing up the dirt. He pounded on the steering wheel. "Why are these assholes chasing me?"

While the pickup was falling back, the Humvee was gaining on him. From what he knew of the army vehicles, they topped out somewhere under one hundred miles per hour. He looked at his speedometer; the needle had just passed one hundred fifteen. The Humvee had been modified for performance.

Seb shifted into fourth then fifth gear and floored it. Keyed up, his mind ran over all the reasons Earl's little clan might have wanted him. His thoughts kept drifting toward that old Wes Craven movie. *Wasn't it set in these hills?*

"Yes!" He was increasing the distance between him and the Humvee. Though someone big—had to be Malcolm—was standing in the turret, he wasn't firing. *They must want me alive.*

Dust kicked up and covered his windshield, so much that he had to flip on his wipers. The water turned the dirt to mud and smeared it in rainbow-shaped streaks. As his view cleared, he could make out a path straight through the mountains at his two o'clock. He adjusted his course and headed for it.

The Humvee screeched to a stop behind him, and he breathed a sigh of relief. *Thump.* Something hit the front of his car. No, something was *on* the hood of his car.

It looked like a massive wad of black bird shit, a long string of it still attached to some far-off bird. *What the hell is it attached to?* Seb leaned over the steering wheel for a closer look. "What the fuck?"

The thick black rope attached to the wad went taught, and the car began to spiral. He turned the wheel hard right, and the Charger glided sideways over the sand, as if on ice. He was lucky the ground was smooth and flat, or he'd surely have flipped.

Rapid-fire bursts sounded to his left. "That asshole's actually shooting at me!" Seb tried to keep his head down while maintaining some semblance of control over the car.

With a snap, the Charger spun free, centrifugal force whipping it around until Seb was facing the wrong direction, wheels spinning one way but the car's momentum slinging it in the other.

EIGHT CYLINDERS

He began to slow. A loud thump like that of a tree falling came from behind him. The back end of his Charger collided with something big, and he rocketed into the dashboard, banging his head against the windshield before whiplashing back into his seat.

He groaned as a trickle of blood ran down his forehead. It dripped off his brow and onto his pants. As his head began to clear, he adjusted his rearview mirror, knocked askew during the collision. He expected to see a giant boulder or a telephone pole or something in it, but instead saw nothing but another black wad and dust covering a splintered rear windshield.

And a shadow of something big rising behind it.

Every nerve in his body screamed danger. The car idled, an easy target, so he hit the gas, letting the wheels catch as more gunfire sounded.

Shit, I'm headed straight at them. But Malcolm wasn't firing anywhere near him. He was aiming much too high and off to Seb's right to hit the car.

A shriek like the scraping of metal against metal reverberated through the air, as if bellowed from the bottom of a well. It varied in pitch and was loud enough to rupture an eardrum, and Seb double-checked whether all his windows were down. The sound was so unearthly that even someone of Seb's generally unflinching character writhed in his own skin.

His palms grew sweaty as sight gave origin to sound. In his side mirror, he caught a glimpse of something he could not comprehend: a cylindrical vine as thick as a redwood, smooth and striated pinkish purple, undulating like a worm caught in the sun. As it rose higher, a white underside became exposed. Circular pads covered the white surface, pulsating like soft coral.

Seb's throat went dry. He stared, mouth agape until the wail of a horn shook him out of it. He faced forward and swerved, preventing a collision with the pickup. Again, he checked his side mirror. The Humvee and pickup turned to follow as he sped back to the small camp in the middle of nowhere.

Some of the shock wore off by the time Seb exited his car. He clenched his fists to try to stop his hands from shaking. His mind juggled one insane explanation after another, never landing on a single rationale for what he'd just seen that made even a smidgen of sense. His confusion made him angry, and he stormed into the tent, guns drawn and ready to demand answers.

Only Helen was inside, fixing him with a single lost puppy-dog eye. Threatening violence against women didn't jive with his somewhat flexible moral code, but the heat of his temper and the enormous monstrosity he'd only barely seen trampled his decorum. Someone was playing a sick joke on him. Had to be. There was no way what he saw could have been real. No land animal could be that big. *Could it?*

Seb's nostrils flared as he stepped toward Helen. He'd get his answers, one way or another. She would have to do. He aimed his gun at her. "All right. Start talking."

"Ha!" Helen tsked. "Guess you ain't as smart as you think you are." She cackled so exuberantly that Seb's face flushed with warmth.

"Don't you think if we could have just driven out of

here, we all would have done it years ago? None of us want to be here. Who the hell would want to be here?" She snorted and waved off his gun as if it were a pesky fly buzzing at her ear.

Seb lowered his gun. "Years? How long have you been here?"

Helen looked up and pursed her lips. Her brow furrowed, and she stared at the ceiling. "I . . . I can't remember. A long time, I think." She rested her chin on her hand and sighed as if the attempt to remember had drained the life out of her. Her eyes stared off into space.

Seb waited on her to snap back to the here and now. As he did, he eyed her from head to toe, trying to get whatever read he could from her T-shirt featuring some band called "The Dead Milkmen," worn loose over baggy jeans tucked into black combat boots. A chain hung from a spiked belt at her side. She reminded him of an eighties punk rocker. Given that she looked in her sixties, Seb thought it kind of made sense. But she couldn't have been in that hellhole for forty years.

Still staring into space, Helen broke her silence. "I was . . . so angry back then. I would've hated you just . . . for the color of your skin." She looked away. "I'm not proud of it. I'm not proud of a lot of things." She pointed at her empty socket. "You know how they say, 'You should see the other guy'? Well, what we did . . . what *I* did to those innocent people . . . it . . . it was unforgivable." Her voice quivered. Her one eye shimmered. "I was so full of hate, such a waste of life. I deserve what happened to my eye." She spread her arms wide. "I deserve this."

Seb crossed his arms. "Lady, I ain't no priest, and I surely ain't no saint. I mean, I've only been here a few days, and that's already staying longer than I planned to. Who we were, what we've done . . . none of that shit matters. What matters is—"

"It's all that matters," Helen muttered.

"What matters," Seb said a little louder, "is how we get the fuck out of here." He frowned. Helen was a dried-up husk of a woman who'd clearly never been decent. But at least she once had hate, anger, and drive. However misdirected her emotions might once have been, Seb could have used that to propel them forward. Now, the tired old woman might as well have been dead. She'd be no use to him. She'd given up years ago.

Will any of them be useful? He needed to get back to Gemma. He needed to get home before Ling—

"Son." Earl's big voice boomed behind him. "By now, you must see there ain't no getting out of here."

Seb turned to face Earl, Angelique, and Red. "That's bullshit! If we can get in, we can get out. Y'all got here somehow, didn't you?" He pointed at each in turn. "How did you get here? How 'bout you?"

Angelique's lips parted, but she said nothing. Red just shook his head.

Something wet tickled Seb's hand, and he looked down to see Juke at his side. He calmed a little as he patted the coyote, who, unlike the rest of them, seemed happy Seb was still alive.

"You think you're the only one to pull a stunt like that?" Earl asked. He jammed a stubby finger into Seb's chest. "You were one of the lucky ones. Most don't get second chances."

Red held up his hand, showing off the cauterized remnants of his pinky and ring finger. "Real lucky, I'd say. At least you came back whole, kid."

Seb straightened, but his voice cracked. "That . . . thing . . . did that to you?"

"Yeah, that inky shit is like battery acid, except way worse. It burns slow, but damn does it hurt! It landed on my handlebar and just the very tips of my finger. When I felt the burn, I panicked so hard that I dumped my bike. I didn't like mistreating 'ol Betsy, but the fall saved my life. Snapped off the pads of my two fingers and kept me from getting too far in. As soon as that monster started to drag away my ride, I thought I was a goner. Malcolm shot that inky shit off the handlebar, but the tiny bit on my fingers kept spreading. I lifted my bike, and I turned right the fuck around. That black goop had eaten off half my fingers by the time I got back, and I ain't too proud to say I was in tears. Not even the kidney stone I'd passed hurt that bad, and that felt like a porcupine had burrowed a den in my dickhole. I was practically begging Doc here to cut my fingers off."

Earl nodded. "If we hadn't, there's no telling if that goop ever would have stopped spreading." He sighed. "That's the best intel we've been able to get on those suckers yet, though. Red here's the only one ever to be touched by that thing and live to tell the tale." He patted the biker on the back, as if turning tail were a badge of honor.

Didn't I do the same thing? Seb studied his shoes. After a moment in silence, he spoke the question he'd dreaded asking since he saw the shadow of the thing that stopped his car dead. "What was it?"

Earl let out a long breath. "We don't know. Some sort of animal, or animals, I guess, if you can believe that." His chin dipped. "Oh, fuck that. Let's call a spade a spade. If King Kong's a monster . . . if Godzilla's a friggin' monster, then that *thing* out there's a goddamn monster! It's like something out of a nightmare, only we're all dreaming it together."

Red put a hand on Earl's shoulder. Whatever circumstances had brought them there, they were all in it together. "You've already seen about as much of it as we have," the biker said. "From what Earl told me on the way over here, you got up close and personal with it. Sticky black elastic goop tethered to something with the horsepower of a thousand Harleys. Tentacles as big as freight trains dropping out of the sky. Goddamn monster is right."

"Tentacles?" Seb swallowed something bitter. "There's more than one?"

"We've seen eight or nine of those arms at a time. Not sure if they belong to one creature or many, but they're all around us. Those of us who tried the mountains on foot in other directions were whisked away before they could even reach the foothills. Sometimes we let a newbie try, just to see if they're still out there." Red coughed and hurriedly added, "After full disclosure, of course."

Earl rolled his eyes. "Not that anyone ever believes us. You see, those tentacles come out of caves you might have noticed when you were out there. The black shit, too. What they're attached to . . . well, you'd have to go inside one of them caves to find out, son."

Angelique rattled off what sounded like a series of curses in Spanish. She shoved a finger at Seb. "*Puto!*

EIGHT CYLINDERS

You are a stupid, stupid man." She spat. "Waste of bullets."

Seb raised an eyebrow. "So you do speak English? I was wondering—"

"Yes, I speak English. Just not to you, *cabron*."

Seb thought better of questioning the logic of her statement. Instead, he diverted his focus to the artillery. "You've got a Humvee, and it's heavily armed. Is there a military base nearby?"

A hundred late-night sci-fi flicks came to mind. He snapped his fingers. "Are we dealing with some Area Fifty-One bullshit here? This the fucking government's doing?" Seb paused, caught his breath, and tried to articulate the idea he was forming. "We could use the Humvee—"

"Forget it," Earl said. "It belongs to Malcolm. He's not . . . all right in the head. PTSD, I suspect. Happens to a lot of vets, good people and some good friends of mine. But when he rolled in here with that thing, we thought we were saved. You know, the Army's here to save us and all that. As it turned out, he just moseyed on in here, scrambled and confused like the rest of us. Something about them mountains screws with the short-term memory." He tapped his head. "Bores holes in the brain. Skeeter thinks it's radiation."

Angelique crossed her arms. "It's not radiation."

Earl shrugged. "Anyway, you're not taking the Humvee. If or when we try to make a run for it, that beast will have Malcolm riding it. And as you saw today, there's nobody else you'd want on it."

"You must have other rides—"

"We've got all kinds of rides, kid," Red said. "Nobody walked in here, except maybe Mary. She's been here the longest."

Seb raised both eyebrows at that. *How's that even possible if she's like twelve and Helen's—*

"They're right on the other side of the partition." Red nodded toward the flap Angelique had entered through earlier with their lunch. "Skeeter's probably wiping them down now. We took the liberty of rolling your charger in there, too. We can check out the damage later. Both Earl and Skeeter are decent mechanics."

Angelique snarled. "Or Mr. *Cabron* can hop back in it and use up his second chance right now."

"Easy," Earl said. "Don't you remember how you were when you got here?"

"You know I can barely remember anything, same as the rest of you. This place, it's like . . . " She clenched her teeth then fired off another string of Spanish phrases Seb assumed were not taught in school.

"I can't stay here." Seb bit his lip, thinking of Gemma. "I have someone waiting for me on the other side of those mountains, and I intend to get back to her. Don't you have people waiting for you?"

Melancholy washed over the faces of all three. Helen, who still sat quietly at the table, rested her head on her arms. What Seb saw in them made his heart twinge with a sense of loss and something more terrifying than the creature itself.

Hopelessness.

Angelique touched his arm, surprising him with her sudden gentleness. "Whoever we had . . . whoever *you* had . . . they aren't waiting any longer."

No.

He jerked away from her touch. That was not acceptable. "There's no life for me here."

Earl shifted on his feet. "At least it's a life—"

"Not for me!"

Red spoke softly. "There are a few graves out back for others who opted out."

Angelique's spitfire returned. "That's the coward's way out."

Red ignored her. "I get it. We've all thought about it. We've got guns. It'd be as easy as pulling a trigger, and for most of us, that wasn't ever hard. But going back out there"—he pointed at the horizon—"that's just trading one form of suicide for another. You haven't seen all that thing can do, the kind of shit that'll make you beg for a bullet. And those of us who disappeared into those caves . . . you haven't heard the screams. I can't unhear them."

"I'm going." Seb set his jaw. "Better to die in those mountains than to waste away here. Any of you who want to come with me are welcome. It seems to me we'd all have a better chance if we went together, with that Humvee laying down some cover."

Earl stroked his chin. "It's been proposed before, and it's always vetoed. But if you'd like, we'll let you state your case to the group tomorrow then put it to a vote. I can't say how much weight a newbie's opinions will have with this crowd, but you're welcome to try. Just don't get your hopes up."

He slapped Seb on the arm. "Why not take the night to think about whether, after what you've seen today, that's something you really want to do?" He stuck out his hand. "Deal?"

Seb stared at it a second then took it. "All right. Deal."

With nothing more to say, Seb walked out of the

tent. Heat swaddled him, close and confining. Just like that place: an open expanse of nothingness, yet a prison all the same.

The sun was already low in the sky, casting a deep red glow over the mountains that made them almost look like erupting volcanoes. Or coated in blood. He might have found the view beautiful had he not already had a run-in with a certain resident of those mountains.

"Makes your balls shrivel, don't it? We stand in the valley of 'The Mountains of Madness.'"

Seb jumped. He turned to find Sly behind him, a viper close enough to strike. How the junkie-psycho had gotten the drop on him, Seb couldn't guess. The dude was clearly stealthy, but the day must have affected Seb more than he'd thought to let anyone get that close without noticing him.

It's not every day you go head-to-head with a giant octopus in the desert. He pursed his lips. Octopus? Was that all it was? He'd heard they military had done atomic bomb testing out in the desert near there. Had something Chernobyl-like happened? And through it, had they created an American Godzilla?

Sly's smile was the thin line of the dancing cobra's. "You like Lovecraft?"

"Who?" Seb gave Sly a once-over and sensed no imminent threat. Aside from looking like a junkie in a place that seemed as sober as a Mormon Sacrament, Sly seemed to have little choice but to keep his seediness to himself. *Still, he might have valuable information . . .*

"That old writer." Sly shrugged. "I don't care much for books neither, but that guy's shit was out of this world, especially when you're tripping. What's your poison?"

"Don't got one."

"Man, it's been so long since I got high, you'd think I'd have lost the taste for it. But nope, still craving it, every day." He scratched his elbow. "Anyway, Lovecraft wrote about this big monster-god thing call Cthulhu, tall as a mountain, who basically had squid tentacles for a beard."

Seb tilted his head toward the mountains. "Is that what you think that thing is? Something you read about when you were high?"

"No clue, compadre." Sly whistled. "I doubt it. Like I said, Cthulhu was like some god. That thing out there just seems territorial or hungry. But damn, it sure does like to eat."

"So, an animal then? Just like the rest of us?"

"Oh, it's an animal." Sly winked. "But not like the rest of us." He smiled big, exposing his blackened teeth. "Some of *us* ain't even like the rest of us. Take you, for example."

Seb pondered that for a second and decided he'd had enough of the junkie. He started to walk away.

"Say, friend?" Sly called back to him. "Think I might be able to get that piece back now?"

Seb stopped but didn't turn. He waited to see if Sly would try for the gun, kind of hoping he would.

But Sly stayed put. "Fancy move you pulled on me earlier. Where'd you learn that shit?"

"I've spent a lot of time in rough places." Though his answer was partly true, Seb left out the fact that he'd spent half his adult life and most of his youth in various dojos and gyms, sparring with whomever he could and testing out his newly learned skills on the street. Carlo had been with him the whole way. Not anymore. All the training in the world had been no match for that bullet.

He continued toward the shack he'd awoken in that morning. With a backhand wave, he said, "I think I might hold onto it a bit longer."

As he walked farther away, Sly left him with a parting shot. "Keep it close, friend. Even this camp's a dangerous place at night."

Seb went around the back of his shack to the well around which all the small hovels were located. Mary was there, drinking from a large ladle attached by a rope to a bucket sitting on the stone ring. He waved, but her back was to him. His feet were light as a dancer's in that soundless void.

"Hey," he said softly so as not to frighten her, leaving some space between them.

Mary bolted upright then froze. Slowly, she put the ladle into the bucket and turned. Her face pale, her dark eyes wide, she stared at Seb like one gaping at her oncoming death.

Then she ran. The girl was fast on her feet for one so young and lanky. She was out of Seb's sight before he could blink.

Seb didn't know what to make of the girl, but he gave her no more thought. His throat itched, and he needed water, so he picked up the ladle. He was amazed at how clear and pure the water in that dust bin was and more amazed it hadn't all dried up. The earth around it was cracked and barren. Almost as good as pavement to drive on but absolute hell to try to live upon.

The well's presence was a wonder for which he was grateful, yet he was afraid to question it; if he did, he thought it might vanish like the mirage he feared it could be. He tasted the water, and to his delight, it was not only real but also somehow cooler and more refreshing than it had been before. He drank deep then poured the water over his head, splashed his face, and washed where he could.

The water below him was still, its surface dark and its depth incalculable. He stared into its abyss, letting his mind drift and his cares evaporate with the droplets rolling off his chin. He was tired. So tired. The bucket beside him was like a foreign object. Where had it come from? He leaned closer to the hole. The shadow of a man stared back from the mirrored surface. Half his head was missing.

"C-Carlo!" Seb jumped back, water rocketing out of his nose and mouth.

Juke licked his hand, the coyote's sudden appearance beside him simultaneously surprising and comforting. He stroked the animal behind its ear, then chanced a peek back into the well. Carlo's reflection was gone.

Juke cocked his head toward the bucket, and Seb held out the ladle so the coyote could drink. Juke lapped up three ladles full before he'd had his fill, licking his lips and nose as he finished.

Seb headed back to the shack, already dry by the time he got there. Juke followed at his heels. Seb collapsed on the cart, still stained with his blood, and rested his head. Juke curled up on the floor beside him.

He was so tired, his mind . . . not clear. *How?*

Carlo? His eyelids fluttered. He thought he had seen Carlo, but laying down now, he began to doubt if his partner's appearance had been real at all. *The heat, that was it. A hallucination.* The heat had sapped his energy, taken his fight, and caused him to see things that were not there.

But Gemma? She was still out there . . . waiting for him.

Isn't she?

Struggling to keep her image behind his eyelids, he fell asleep.

CHAPTER 4

SEB AWOKE TO screaming.

Juke whimpered at the door. After one look back, clearly wanting Seb to follow, he nuzzled open the door and stepped into the night.

Seb leapt out of bed and pulled on his pants. Shirtless and shoeless, he grabbed both handguns from beneath his pillow and raced in the direction of a growing crowd. Skeeter and Helen were beside him, each half-dressed and newly awakened.

"It came from Angelique's place," Skeeter said through heavy breaths. The scrappy little shit was fast and armed. He led the way across the circle, toward the shack opposite Seb's, a double-barrel shotgun in hand.

A weaselly voice came from inside. It belonged to Sly. "You ain't gonna shoot—"

A single gunshot split the air, bringing Seb's group skidding to a halt. Skeeter pump-loaded the chamber of his shotgun and looked to Seb for guidance. Helen shrugged and showed her empty hands. Seb handed her Sly's pistol and readied his own. With a finger over his lips, he signaled for the other two to circle left around the plywood structure while he circled right.

They all made it to the door at the same time. It was slightly ajar.

"What's going on?" Earl asked between wheezes, his face red and his pants open beneath his large belly. Gasping for air, he added, "What's happened?" Red hobbled up behind him, while Malcolm watched stoically from a few feet away.

Seb held out a hand, palm down with fingers spread. Everyone froze. He held up his pistol and grabbed his wrist with his other hand, as he'd seen the cops do both times they'd arrested him, then kicked in the door. As it swung open, he backed behind the door frame to the relative safety of the plywood wall.

He peeked around the corner, into the room. Into darkness.

Seb could hear breathing, but he saw nothing. The door had ricocheted off the other side of the wall and was slowly closing. He propped it open with his foot and carefully pushed it.

The moonlight through the doorway illuminated the figure of a woman, kneeling in the center of the room, wearing only her bra and underwear—Angelique. *Is she crying?*

A child, who had to be Mary, curled her arms around Angelique's waist and nestled her head in her lap. Juke rested against the girl, but he lifted his head as Seb approached.

Angelique's lip was split and trickled blood. A small bump had risen on her forehead. With one hand, Angelique stroked the child's head. With her other hand, she leveled a gun at Seb. It shook in her grip.

Seb lowered his gun slowly then tucked it away. His arms raised, he took a step into the room then another, then another. If the coyote was protecting them, he showed no sign of aggression. Slowly, gently, Seb covered Angelique's hand with his own. She didn't resist as he took the gun away from her.

Earl shuffled into the room, his chest heaving, his arms swinging. "Mary? Is she okay?"

Helen grabbed his arm and held him back. After handing the gun back to Seb, she crouched by Angelique and tried to help her up.

"No," the little girl muttered. Her arms tightened around Angelique, and she wiped her tears against the young woman's thigh.

"Angelique," Helen said softly, stepping deeper into the room. She put her arm around the other woman. "Tell us what happened. Are you and Mary okay?"

Angelique sobbed. "It . . . it was Sly. He snuck in here to . . . hurt Mary. He roughed me up a bit to get to her. I guess he thought he'd knocked me out, and almost had, 'cause he put his gun down and went after the child, the sick fuck! Christ! She's only twelve!"

She unleashed a volley of Spanish slurs at a speed Seb hadn't a chance of catching, then paused and let out a breath. "He had her cornered. His hands . . . *dios!* I grabbed his gun and shot him."

"Just how many guns do you people have?" Seb looked at the two in his hands and the third in his belt. Since he'd gotten there, he'd accrued a small arsenal.

"Shh," Helen said. Seb didn't know if it was meant to shut him up or soothe the child.

"Did he . . . do anything to her?" Earl asked.

"No, thank God," Angelique said. "But she saw what he did to me. She . . . she knew what he wanted."

"That son of a bitch," Skeeter said, pushing his way into the room. "He'd better be dead, 'cause if he isn't, I'm gonna kill him. Where is he—"

Skeeter thumped onto the floor, tripping over the limp and prone form of Sly. "Found him," he said, popping back up to his feet, face reddening. He gave Sly a swift kick to the ribs. Apparently, he felt a few more kicks were needed to make sure Sly was dead, because his leg swung again and again.

Seb walked over to the body and put a hand out, gently signaling for Skeeter to stop. He rolled Sly onto his back. The dead man's head squelched as it turned, the back of it soaked in blood. The bullet had entered Sly's forehead near his temple and made a messy exit. In the mess, Seb saw only a reminder of what had happened to Carlo.

"Let's feed him to the creature tomorrow," Malcolm said in his low baritone that was both menacing and authoritative. "He doesn't deserve to be buried here."

"Now hold on a sec," Red said. "Maybe we should consider, you know, the meat value."

Seb let out his breath as the crowd released a collective groan. *Well, at least they're not cannibals, yet.* He again recalled that Wes Craven movie.

"What?" Red threw up his hands. "Just a thought, sheesh."

"Come on, Skeeter," Earl said. "Help me get him out of here." He grabbed Sly under the knees.

"Why do I have to get the gross side?" Skeeter whined, but he picked up the dead man under his arms, anyway. The others made way as the two carried the body out of the shack. They barely made it more than twenty feet when they swung Sly and tossed him like garbage into the dirt at the outskirts of the tiny settlement. They dusted off their hands, turned, and made their way back to Seb, who had watched the scene with solemn amusement.

When Seb looked into the shack, Helen was washing the blood off Angelique's face and offering her own home to the woman and Mary for the night. The others were already dispersing.

"Come on," Earl said, patting Seb on the back. "Ain't nothing more to see here."

Seb hesitated by the door. "Will the girl be okay?"

"I don't know, son." Earl shook his head. "Will any of us ever be?"

The events of the day hung on Seb as heavy as his sweat. As he started back to his bed, he called Juke, but the coyote wouldn't come. Together with the little girl, both of them standing outside the door to Angelique's home, Juke watched him leave, his head hung low. The girl watched him, too, her face turned up into a scowl, her eyes full of fire.

Not for the first time, Seb wondered how a little girl like her had ended up in a place like that. And why she seemed to have so much contempt for him.

"All right, boy," he called to Juke. "You stand guard."

He turned to leave.

CHAPTER 5

HIS SLEEP WAS restless. Tossing and turning, he dreamed of Gemma, the shoot-out, his dead partner's bloodless face and glassy eyes. He wondered if maybe he would have been better off if he had died there with Carlo. He dreamed of all the wrong choices he'd made in life—the robberies, the drug deals gone bad, the faces of the men he'd killed, men who'd had it coming—but also of the good things, the parts of life that had truly made it worth living.

He dreamed of that way station, of its people, not all good and not all bad, of the little girl, Mary, and of the community they'd built out of necessity that had somehow grown into something more. With the exception of Sly, who was dead anyway, they actually seemed to care about one another.

Seb had someone he cared for, too. She was miles away and, thanks to him, in a shitload of trouble. He would make another go of it in the morning, with or without the rest of them. He had to. He had to get out.

"How you doing, buddy?" a familiar voice asked, breaking through the transient vividness of dreamscapes.

Seb jolted at the sound. His eyes, slowly coming

into focus, took in the scene. He was in the shack, in bed, a figure sitting in the shadow at the foot of it.

He propped himself up on his elbows and blinked. "Carlo?"

"It's me, buddy." Carlo leaned forward, his face moving into a sliver of moonlight stealing through the crack in the door.

Seb was relieved to find his friend's face whole again. It was Carlo all right—easy smile, bushy eyebrows, prominent chin—all Carlo right down to the mole on his cheek.

All Carlo, except the eyes. They were solid black, like onyx.

"Are you okay?"

"Of course not." Carlo laughed. "I'm dead, and we don't have much time."

"But—"

"You're dreaming, buddy."

"Then what are you?" Seb grimaced. "Where are you?"

"You know." Carlo winked and made a clicking noise with his mouth. "You wouldn't have asked the question if you didn't." He leaned closer, his dark-pool eyes endless caverns into unknown realms, hiding unspeakable horrors. They reminded Seb of the mountains and that horror residing in its caves.

"But the more important question is: Where are you?"

"I . . . I got out of the city. Just flew out of there like a bat out of hell. No plan. No place to go. I was so out of it, I think I used Ling's eye of all things to guide me out of there. Can you imagine that?" Seb chuckled then looked away from those abysmal, damning eyes, suddenly ashamed. "I wouldn't have left you behind. You gotta know that, Carlo. It's just that . . . you know . . . "

"I was dead?"

"Yeah."

"It's cool, bro. Ling can't do shit to me that he hasn't already. My fate is sealed, though right now, I'm risking making it a whole lot worse. Just . . . listen to me. Look out for those people. Look out for that little girl."

"I can't stay here. I have to get back to—"

Carlo, not one usually prone to anger, leapt to his feet. "It's too late for Gemma!" He growled, paced, then sat back down. He slapped the bed. "Did you ever consider you might just be exactly where you're supposed to be? And let me tell you, there are far worse places than this!" He shuddered and looked away as if he might cry. In all the years Seb had known him, he'd never seen Carlo cry. Carlo took a deep breath and slumped. "Don't be stupid, Seb. It's too late for Gemma. Don't make it too late for you."

A screech shook the air outside. Seb didn't recognize the sound, but it chilled his blood all the same.

It affected Carlo worse. He jumped up again, his face white as snow, his eyes leaking black-oil tears. "I gotta go." Trembling, he turned and ran for the door.

"Wait!" Seb kicked the sheet off his legs. "What do you mean it's too late for Gemma?" He hopped out of bed and started after his friend, his arms reaching for him just as Carlo passed through the solid wood of the door.

Outside, the shriek came again. This time, it was closer.

CHAPTER 6

THE SOUND OF a scream sent Seb lurching up in bed for the second time that night. Only this time, he knew it didn't belong to the living. He whispered a prayer for Carlo. Dream or no dream, it felt real enough to him.

He pulled the sheet up to his chin and lay back down, his hand smearing a dot of what looked like ink into the linen. When he finally crawled out of bed, he felt as if he hadn't slept at all. His muscles ached. His mouth, though dry, was heavy with the taste of vomit. His head throbbed where it had smacked into his windshield. Worse still, his side felt as though it had been stabbed, the knife still carving circles inside him. When he checked the bandages, he saw that a spot of blood had soaked through them.

He needed to clean the wound and rewrap it. But more pressing, he needed to piss. He dressed as quickly as he could, considering the ache in every movement, then shambled to the door.

When he stepped outside, the heat and light bombarded him like a juggernaut. He threw an arm up to shield his eyes from the sun, already several degrees above the horizon, and the wicked mountains that loomed there. A rumble of voices came from the tent nearby. He turned around, unzipped his fly, and pissed against his shack.

The act was short but satisfying, and he headed to the well to replenish his reserves. He washed up as best he could, removing his shirt and dumping a full bucket over his head. As he scrubbed his pits, he glanced over at the edge of camp where Earl and Skeeter had disposed of Sly. The body was gone. He wondered if some predator had taken it away during the night. He shivered, thinking of that thing in the mountains, wondering what people tasted like to calamari. Then, he circled back to the tent to see what commotion had been stirred up that morning.

He shook off his dream and Carlo's words. He had to believe Gemma was still out there. Ling wouldn't kill her, not as long as he thought he could use her to get to Seb. Ling would hurt her, though. He would hurt her real bad.

No, Seb had to leave, and his odds were better if the others left with him. He prepared his speech in his head as he walked over. Convincing those yokels to chance an escape wouldn't be easy. None of them wanted to be there, but some of them would surely die if they tried to leave.

So long as it's not me. He smirked then frowned. Trying to convince himself he was a tough loner had failed. With the exception of Carlo, he had been exactly that on the other side of the mountains. Until he found Gemma, who'd made him feel something more. Feeling, the ability to actually give a damn about someone other than himself, once released, wasn't easy to lock away again.

EIGHT CYLINDERS

And it spread like a cancer. For some reason, he cared for the little community in which he'd found himself. Some of them, anyway. Earl had saved his life then, with the help of Skeeter and Malcolm, saved his life a second time. Maybe it wasn't fair to ask them to risk their lives. Seb knew how to drive. He'd been outrunning and outmaneuvering cops since he was fifteen. And he sort of knew what he was up against. Well, at least he wasn't going in blind like last time.

As he entered the tent, thinking he'd be going it alone and hoping Malcolm would, at minimum, provide some firepower from a safe distance, everyone hushed. All eyes turned toward him. Confused, he stared back.

"We're going," Earl said after a moment in silence. "Well, everyone except Helen."

The old woman huddled into herself. "I belong here."

Seb's confusion must have shown on his face, because Skeeter blurted, "It's Mary. She left the camp last night by herself."

Seb froze. "What are we doing?" He clapped. "Let's get after her."

Earl rose. "It's okay. She's back. Angelique followed her trail last night and brought her back safely . . . sort of."

"What do you mean 'sort of'?"

Earl nodded behind him. Curled in the dust in the tent's corner, Angelique held the child, Juke again having found his way to their side. "She won't wake up. Angelique found her that way, about a mile out, just lying in the dirt. We thought maybe she was just exhausted, but every attempt to wake her has failed."

Angelique looked up, her eyes accusing them all, weeping as she cradled Mary in her arms. The small girl's chest rose and fell, but she didn't stir.

Seb's heart might have broken had his years not so hardened it. Still, a hodgepodge community of thieves and junkies and, he suspected, murderers were all banding together behind a little girl, willing to risk their lives for her. It was far more than he'd come to expect from others. Had they developed a sense of kinship birthed out of necessity? Or was there more to it than that?

And is their readiness to leave even necessary? Mary was sound asleep, sure, but otherwise, she looked healthier than the rest of them put together. "What's wrong with her?"

"We don't know," Earl said. "She's not responding to any external stimuli. I can't find a damn thing wrong with her, but no matter what I do, I can't get so much as a finger twitch out of her."

"We don't have proper care for her," Angelique added. "She needs a real doctor." She clenched her teeth. "She deserves a real life."

Seb shrugged. "But I mean, she could wake up, right?"

"And if she doesn't?" Earl asked. "She won't last much more than a day without water in this heat. We can keep trying to pour it down her throat, maybe engineer some kind of IV, but it's doubtful that would work, and it won't be anything close to sterile. In trying to help her, we may just make things worse. And it's not like we've got medicine or antibiotics."

"What Doc's trying to say," Red added, "is that we've all agreed that this ain't no place for a little girl to grow up. I think we've all felt that and known that for a long time. The rest of us might deserve this place, but she sure as hell don't. We just needed a swift kick in the ass to do something about it." He looked away, then sucked in a breath and met Seb's stare. "After seeing the way you handled yourself under sudden and unimaginable pressure yesterday, we'd like you to get her out of here."

Malcolm grunted and nodded.

Seb was taken aback. "Won't the Humvee be her best—"

"Malcolm and I will be in the Humvee," Earl said, "providing cover like yesterday. All of the other drivers will fan out. We'll give that beast as many targets as possible."

Angelique sniffed and cast him a hopeful stare. "You'd better look out for her. Promise us you'll do right by her."

Seb's heart did actually break a little then. His promise came unbidden. "I will."

"All right, then." Red clapped him on the shoulder. "What are we waiting for?"

"What? Now?" Seb raised an eyebrow. He scanned the group. "This instant?"

"Ain't no time like the present, son," Earl said.

"Shouldn't we wait until dark? Try to sneak past that thing at night?"

"No, man," Skeeter answered. "That thing don't sleep, and it sees us just as well at night as it does during the day. Or smells us. I'm not really sure which. Problem is, at night, it can see us, but we can't see it."

Skeeter bounced on his feet, his body trembling and his voice cracking, but he was keeping his shit together. Seb's face flushed with warmth. He hoped he could keep his shit together, too.

We're doing this, he thought, rubbing his palms together. *We're really doing this.*

He looked at the girl and frowned. He'd never been responsible for anyone but himself, yet somehow, a little girl's fate was now in his hands. It wasn't something he'd wanted or asked for, and he couldn't understand why these people were placing their faith and trust in him. He hadn't ever been worthy of anyone's faith and trust, except maybe from Carlo and Gemma, and look where that had landed both of them.

She ain't my problem. Seb gritted his teeth at the thought, a tinge of anger swelling within at the burden thrust upon him. But he quickly subdued it, having resigned himself to the task as soon as it had been proposed. He would do everything he could for the girl, even if it meant sacrificing his car or even himself.

If I'm brave enough. He sighed. He knew what kind of man he was, the kind of man he'd always been: selfish, reckless, maybe a bit crazy. *Crazy enough to try this? I've never been the hero type.*

His shoulders drooping, he said, "Put her in my car and strap her in good. It's going to be one hell of a ride."

After some resistance, Red took Mary from Angelique and carried her through the opening to the adjacent room. Angelique and the others, all except Helen, followed. Seb brought up the rear.

At the flap, Seb stopped and turned back to Helen. "Are you sure you won't come?"

She slowly shook her head. "There's nothing left for me out there."

"There's nothing for you here, either."

"I belong here."

Seb frowned. This wasn't his battle to fight. He slipped through the opening.

He'd expected to see vehicles on the other side, but he wasn't prepared for their number or condition. His mouth dropped open. "Holy shit!"

Immediately in front of him, Skeeter stood with a rag in hand, dusting off a customized Shelby Edition Ford F-150 with a black monster of a souped-up V-8 engine shining from meticulous care under the open hood. White gloss paint, chrome rims, and tires that looked like they belonged on a tractor, affixed to wheels on jacked-up axles, the truck was both beauty and beast. Smoothed flat against its doors were decals of the same naked female silhouette that danced provocatively on Skeeter's hat.

The vehicle was in pristine condition, not a speck of dust on it. It was proof of a bond between man and machine that Seb understood better than most.

Skeeter threw a thumb over his shoulder, a greasy rag hanging from his grip. "Your baby's down that way. We banged out the dents as best we could. Didn't see any damage to the chassis, thankfully. Oh, and we added a little something something." He winked. "Hope you don't mind."

To the left of the pickup sat the beat-up truck Skeeter had driven the day before. If it had an owner, he or she was not present, and Seb didn't think it polite to ask. He did wonder why, if Skeeter had that much nicer Ford, he had taken a rusted piece of shit—one that looked like it might break down at any second—to stop Seb from leaving.

His confusion must have been written all over his face. Laughing, Skeeter said, "You didn't think I'd waste *my* truck trying to save your sorry ass, did you?"

Seb shrugged. With the way that creature attacked cars, he supposed Skeeter's comment made sense.

Beyond the rusty pickup was a Volkswagen Beetle, the Humvee with Malcolm already standing in its turret, what Seb thought might be a brown IROC, and a black Chevelle Super Sport, 1969 model if Seb had to guess. This latter vehicle was a beauty to behold. All black except for its silver trimmings, the muscle car had all the weight and momentum of a two-ton cannonball and would be just as deadly at top speed. Its windows were tinted darker than pitch. Seb couldn't help admiring it, but he'd take his Charger's handling and dependability over it any day—especially on that day, when he would need it most.

When his hands were on the Charger's steering wheel, he and it were one. He couldn't think of another vehicle, except maybe a tank, that he would rather rely on to barrel through a nasty situation—like dodging giant tentacles.

He took a deep breath and headed for his car. On his way, he passed Angelique, who had fitted a dune buggy with sharpened junk-metal shards that jutted from the roll bars and the bumpers. The makeshift blades were the size of swords, nearly as big as the buggy's shocks. Desert camouflaged with big bloated wheels, it looked like something out of a *Mad Max* movie. It would handle great if the terrain got rough, but Seb doubted it topped out over one hundred miles per hour.

When Angelique noticed him, she ran over and

hugged him. The act seemed so out of character for her that Seb was momentarily caught off guard. He stood with his arms out, not knowing whether to push her away or hug her back.

She let go before he could decide. "Help her," she begged, "and I'll do all I can to help you." Her cheeks wet, she turned away, unable to look him in the eye any longer.

Seb nodded and kept walking. Red revved the engine of his Harley Davidson. The bike was a cherry-red Road King, beautiful and fast but heavy and a little clumsy, a cruiser and not the fastest or easiest to maneuver of its kind. Seb noticed that the end of one handlebar had been welded on.

Seb whistled. "A fine hog, Red, but maybe not your best choice for survival." Seb looked past him, and his brow furrowed. *Particularly when several dirt bikes and ATVs are sitting at the far end of the tent, all of which look to be in good shape.*

Red laughed. "Don't let my girl here fool you, kid. Yeah, she might be a little wide and carry a few extra pounds, but she purrs like a kitten and roars like a lion. Runs like one, too. There ain't no Betsy I'd rather be riding. Besides, if I'm going to die out there, at least it'll be while doing what I love most, taking this ol' gal for a spin." He donned a helmet, visor up, the mouth of a grinning skull painted over it, then extended his hand. "Good luck out there, kid."

"See you on the other side." They shook hands, and Seb wondered if he'd ever speak to Red or any of them again.

Earl was leaning against the Charger, his arms crossed, when Seb approached. "'Bout freakin' time," he said, fixing Seb with a cold glare. Then he smiled. "Mary's in back, ready to go. She's got a helmet, but try not to slam her around too much, will ya? If you have to evacuate, you'd better be taking her with you, or I swear to God, I'll run you down myself. I assume you know how to unbuckle your own seat belt?" He pointed to the strap around Mary's waist.

Seb nodded.

"Look here." Earl moved to the front window, reached in, and pulled out a pressurized canister with an injector tube that coiled under the dash. "We gave you an extra boost. Nitrous. We stole most of a kit from this a-hole with some decked-out piece of Japanese plastic before its owner could drive it out of here. Good for us, uh, bad for its owner. He and his car are up in those caves now, and I feel a smidgen of guilt wondering if he might have made it had he had this baby still intact." He spat. "Doubtful. The fucker couldn't drive for shit. Anyway, his loss, our gain, 'cept what we didn't take, we had to invent. The way we've jury-rigged it, bypassing the intake manifold and opting for a direct port injection, it's just as bound to blow up your engine as it is to propel you forward."

Earl grabbed his arm and leaned in close. "Son, I'm serious. Skeeter, Red, and I combined make one damn good mechanic, but that shit's volatile, custom-made, and from a rather questionable source. It shouldn't harm you, but it could flatline your car. And out there, that's as good as dead. So use it only if you have to." He huffed. "I think you'll have to. You're gonna need that and all the luck you can get. We all will."

He squeezed Seb's arm and turned to walk away.

"Hey, Earl," Seb said.

"Something else you need, son?" He forced a smile. "I ain't one for goodbyes."

"Thanks."

"Don't mention it. Just ride like the devil or, better yet, like the devil's on your ass, 'cause he's gonna be." He turned then turned back again. "Oh, and follow my lead."

Seb reached for the door handle, and at once, Juke was at his side, pushing to get in. "Sorry, boy," Seb said, squeezing in front of the coyote and sliding into the front seat. "You don't want any part of where we're going."

Juke whimpered once, cocked his head, then ran into the other room. *Good,* Seb thought. *Stay here with Helen, where it's safe.*

CHAPTER 7

SEB WATCHED AS Red jogged over to the corner of the tent. Red unwrapped the cord that was twisted around a wooden spike, and the tent's side panel loosened and fell.

Engines spurred to life. Seb started the Charger, then waited for a sign to move. With a honk like a trombone, the Humvee ran over the crumpled tarp. One by one, the other vehicles followed.

"Here we go," Seb said. He checked his mirrors and the little girl sleeping in his back seat, envious she wouldn't have to see what was coming. After shifting into reverse, he backed the car out, turned it around, and followed Red out of the tent.

The caravan coasted around to the front of the tent like some low-budget parade of misfit toys. Each vehicle took a position on a side of the Humvee. A spot nearest the military vehicle, at its right, was left open for Seb and the child, Angelique's dune buggy leaving a gap about ten meters wide. Behind the Humvee, on what looked like nothing more than a metal sled affixed to the vehicle by a short length of chain, were two ATVs.

Spares. Seb winced. He hoped no one would need one.

EIGHT CYLINDERS

In his rearview, Helen emerged from the tent. She had what looked like rosary beads in her hand. Was she praying for them?

This group could use all the prayers it can get. Seb wasn't a religious man, but he couldn't help feeling as if he were being tested. So much about that place didn't make sense to him; there were so many things that he felt he ought to be questioning, things that seemed less important the more time he spent there. Like he was missing some bigger picture. The well that didn't dry up. The food, as bad as it was, where nothing else lived or grew. The people themselves and how none of them seemed to know how they got there or when. How he wasn't even sure how he'd gotten there. And the little girl, Mary . . . she didn't seem to fit at all. It was like—

Earl revved his engine.

And Helen fell.

A man stood behind her, something metal glinting in his hand. *Sly? Impossible. I saw his body. He was fucking dead.* Seb had once heard of a man who'd been shot in the temple and survived because the bullet had wrapped around his skull. *Could something like that have happened to Sly? No, that fucker was dead.*

Yet there he was, standing over Helen. She was on her back, one hand pressed tightly against her stomach, the other reaching up to ward off her attacker, rosary beads dangling from her outstretched fingers.

Earl revved his engine a second time.

"No, wait!" Seb fumbled for the switch to power down his window while watching Helen scramble back from Sly on her butt and heels. A streak of fur bolted from the tent. In an instant, Juke had Sly by the wrist, biting and gnashing. Sly's mouth opened wide, likely crying out in pain, the sound unheard under the roar of the engines. The metal object fell from his hand, and he kicked at the coyote. Helen was on her feet then. She ran inside the tent.

Seb checked the windows to his right and left. Did no one else see what was happening?

Earl's tires screeched and spun. The Humvee barreled forward. All the other vehicles took off with it. All except Seb's. He needed to go.

"I'm sorry, Helen," he said, pressing the pedal to the floor. With one last glance in his rearview, he saw Juke running after him. Sly was gone.

"Stay back, buddy. Keep her safe." The dust and dirt his tires kicked up created a mini sandstorm that obscured everything in his rearview. He passed through another cloud of dust and found himself only a foot away from Angelique's vehicle. He adjusted course, positioning himself between the Humvee and the buggy.

One vehicle lurched ahead of the pack. Seb was sufficiently off to the side and out of the pluming sand to make out the F-150. Skeeter was pulling ahead, trying to draw the creature's attention.

They were close to the point where that black gunk had hit his car. Seb looked at the spot on his hood where it had been. The goop was gone—evaporated, he supposed—but it had eaten a small hole through the hood and peeled away a much larger circle of paint. He thought of Red's missing fingers and was happy not to be exposed like the biker and Angelique, her vehicle having no windshield or windows.

The Humvee honked and began to slow. The other vehicles hit their brakes. All except Skeeter's; the F-150 pressed forward.

Something flashed through the air and smacked into the pickup's grille. Seb couldn't believe how fast it had moved. He never saw where it came from, just saw it hit.

But he got a good look at the thing as it set its hook. A string of black mucus trailed from the front end of the F-150 to some point in the mountains Seb couldn't quite make out from over a thousand yards away. The pickup's momentum and the pull of that sticky rope dragged the vehicle forward, despite Skeeter pumping the brakes, the truck's back wheels zigzagging over the sand. He looked like a fish fighting not to be reeled in.

For some reason, Malcolm wasn't shooting. "What the hell, man?" Seb yelled through his open window. "Help him!"

When Malcolm did nothing, Seb grabbed his pistol. He was about to fire when he realized the plan, something they might have thought to clue him in on ahead of time. Skeeter slammed the truck into reverse. The F-150 was no longer moving forward. Mostly, the tires just spun in place, billowing up a whole lot of dust clouds and burning rubber. But every now and then, the tires would catch, and the truck would lurch backward.

The fish became the fisherman. The truck's tires caught for good. Seb didn't know much about the Shelby model of the pickup, but he guessed it had horsepower that rivaled his Hellcat's and a shit-ton of weight behind it, too. Foot by foot, the truck pulled the source of the sticky substance from its hiding place.

The caravan passed Skeeter, creeping onward as he kept the beast distracted. Not sure that he wanted to see but needing to know what he was up against, Seb traced the thick black cable to the mouth of the cave. Something akin to a striated purple-black beak emerged, curved and sharply pointed like that of a giant squid, the opposite end of the black rope tucked somewhere inside it. The beak opened wide, revealing fleshy wriggling masses hanging from its toothless mouth. They were too small to make out from his distance and might as well have been giant bats hanging from the roof of a cave. A cave within a cave, one that was moving, being dragged out into the light. The beast drew closer to Seb as he drew closer to it. Those things in its mouth, clearer now . . . *They almost look like . . .*

People?

The creature shrieked, the sound waves from that horrible, unnatural clatter rattling through the Charger and Seb's nerves. He blocked an ear with one hand while reaching for the window switch with his other. If he somehow managed to live through the day, he doubted his hearing would ever be the same.

As the creature's bellowing stopped, a few of the hanging appendages in its mouth fell. They landed on a rolling, forked black tongue that flicked them down its hatch. Seb heard more screaming then, muffled but voluminous . . . and almost human. *The singing of the damned.* He considered turning back. As he glanced in his rearview, he saw Mary sleeping, experiencing a peace she would never find in her waking hours if she stayed there. He set his jaw and gripped the wheel tighter.

Still, the F-150 pulled. Still, the beak grew in size, already as big as a house. The rock around the cave opening cracked and crumbled, sending boulders avalanching down into the ravine. Fortunately, they landed just outside the path Earl was blazing. The creature the beak belonged to must have been as big as the mountains themselves. How it maneuvered through them, Seb couldn't imagine. Or were the mountains part of its camouflage, like the shell of some monstrous hermit crab?

Seb swallowed hard. His palms slicked the wheel with sweat. It was just some damn animal: big sure, but dumb like any other. *Don't think about it. Keep your eyes and mind on the road.* Sly's words haunted him. *It's an animal but not like the rest of us.*

When Skeeter and the creature came to a standstill, the Humvee shot forward. Seb stepped on his gas. Malcolm opened fire on that gigantic mouth.

The creature cried out with every round Malcolm hit it with. The soldier's aim was impeccable, but the bullets couldn't have been more than mosquito bites to that thing. Still, no other snot rockets came from the other caves. Maybe they only had to fend against one creature after all. Maybe, while Skeeter, Earl, and Malcolm had it occupied, the others could make their—

Thump!

Dust like a mushroom cloud rose miles into the sky. The earth rumbled under Seb's tires, somehow seeming less firm, like cracking ice. He slowed and leaned over the steering wheel, squinting to see through the polluted air. A tentacle danced like a live wire over the ground a half mile ahead of them, having emerged from a cave to the right. It blocked the path of the Humvee, Seb's Charger, and Angelique's buggy, which left the ground with each thump of the massive limb.

Malcolm refocused his fire at the tentacle as the Humvee swerved left. Where it was hit by bullets, the tentacle curled like an inchworm, creating an arch for Seb to pass beneath. The appendage rolled like a wave above him. Its white underside glistened, its suckers pulsating and bursting open like sores, oozing with slime. He gunned it through the opening. Angelique filed in behind him.

Once through, he glanced in his rearview at his charge in the back seat. *Still sleeping?* He smirked. *If that won't wake you up, kid, nothing will.* They were all risking a hell of a lot for a girl who might already be lost, and he prayed Mary was worth it.

To Seb's left, the Humvee and Red's bike circled the tentacle. The F-150 remained behind, still demanding the attention of that ugly beast.

Something huge, the head around the beak, squeezed partly out of the cave. It was not quite fixed in form, like a newborn's head shaped by the narrow orifice through which it was pushed.

More and more, the beast emerged, revolting and maddening to behold. An eye, bloodshot but with yellow veins slithering like serpents over a field of gray. Zombie-like, plague-ridden mottled flesh, living in a constant state of dying, with lavender to charcoal-colored collops teeming with pustules hanging irregularly from its head as if it has showered in acid rain. A pupil as big as a subway tunnel. Something shimmering in its depth reminded Seb of the well. The skin around the eye and beak was almost translucent, bluish spheres beneath it moving like atoms under a microscope.

Seb needed to look away, to keep his eyes on the road, but his terror kept his eyes locked on that monster. It couldn't be real. It didn't belong. It wasn't natural. It just couldn't be.

The beast stopped moving. Seb stared, his mouth tasting something bitter. *Is it stuck?*

A loud twang came from behind, snatching Seb's attention. The truck's grille disappeared into the cave along with the ropelike black substance.

An engine purred, growing louder quickly. An IROC careened toward his bumper. In his mirror, Seb caught a glimpse of Helen slumped over the steering wheel. She didn't appear to be awake, never mind watching the road. And she wasn't turning.

Seb moved out of the IROC's way and let Helen pass, so close she clipped his side mirror with her own, knocking it askew. He reached out to try and fix it. "Oh shit," was all he could say as he faced forward again and saw tentacles falling like skyscrapers from the sky. The IROC slammed into the first one as it touched down, and the tentacle recoiled, the creature shrieking in pain. Helen did not react as the beast's suckers attached to the IROC and carried it and Helen into the air.

Whether intentional or not, Helen's sacrifice had allowed Seb and Angelique to live. The caravan slowed as it approached and passed under the tentacle, having to navigate out of the path of the third tentacle and each other. As he passed beneath the IROC, Seb saw that one of the sucker-pod things had turned gelatinous and spread over the vehicle like a starfish devouring a clam. He prayed Helen was already dead. *But if Helen's here, where's Sly?*

Angelique led the way around the third tentacle, an easy act for Seb to follow as the appendage wasn't moving. He had the odd sense it was lying in wait or had dropped there for the sole purpose of blocking his retreat. Which begged the question: "What joy awaits me up ahead?"

The Humvee made a hard right behind him, nearly taking out Red as it fishtailed. But Red ducked behind the Humvee, then passed it on the opposite side.

Seb threw up a fist to cheer him on but lowered it as black goop smacked down on Red's helmet, that time coming from a cave at the right. The damn creature was mobile, and Red was a dead man. One eye on the road and the other on Red, Seb watched as the biker struggled to remove his helmet. The goop rope went taut before he could.

Had Red not been moving in the direction of the pull, the beast might have ripped his head clean off. Instead, it tore Red from his bike, yanking him twenty feet in the air before Red could undo his chin strap. The biker hit the ground hard and was being pulled through the dirt. Seb rolled down his window and shot at the black gunk with everything he had. Malcolm was dividing rounds between the goop and a new, fourth tentacle casting a shadow over the whole caravan.

Seb slammed on the brakes. Red had somehow gotten his helmet off and was rising to his feet. The biker looked no worse for wear. The son of a bitch was actually smiling.

To his own surprise, so was Seb. He pounded on

his hood and began to reverse. "Run, you crazy bastard!"

Red started his way when a black Chevelle turned and sideswiped him. The collision sent the biker airborne, and he smacked against the soft white underside of the dormant tentacle. As soon as he made contact, Red was screaming, stuck to that monstrosity as if it were human flypaper. He sank into its flesh like a man drowning in quicksand, parts of him dissolving quicker than others.

The Chevelle blazed past him. Seb roared in anger, his knuckles whitening around the steering wheel. He couldn't see through those windows, but he knew who was driving. He didn't know why or how, but he knew who. And he was damn sure that the next time that fucker died, he was going to stay dead.

Seb punched the car back into gear, everyone in front of him now except Skeeter, and Seb didn't know if he was dead or alive. As he turned the corner, Seb passed under the shadow of the fourth tentacle.

"Come on!" Earl yelled, waving him on. He and Malcolm had stayed back to cover him.

No, not me. The girl. What makes this little girl so damn important to them?

Whatever the reason, Seb wasn't about to waste an opportunity. He shifted and maneuvered with the speed and skill of a NASCAR driver, gaining on the Chevelle and Angelique, still a mile up ahead, where the path between the mountains began to narrow.

The way out. He hoped, anyway.

A fifth tentacle hovered gingerly over the trail, as if feeling the air.

Waiting.

Sly slowed, no longer nipping at Angelique's back wheels. Though none of the other vehicles handled as well as the buggy on that terrain, the Chevelle and Seb's Hellcat were both faster. But the cold-blooded killer driving the black muscle car was content to let Angelique poke them a path through.

Malcolm laid down cover fire from somewhere behind them. The man was a godsend. Even from a football field away, he tattooed the fifth tentacle with continuous pinpricks, causing it to recoil.

Seb allowed himself to hope. They were doing it. Their system was working. So far they'd lost only one of their caravan—two if they counted Helen, who was probably already lost to them anyway.

Yeah, like Sly. He frowned. *There's one who doesn't deserve to make it.*

A thunderous crash sounded behind Seb. Tires skidded over dirt. The gunfire stopped.

Malcolm screamed. "Go! Go! Go!"

Seb checked his rearview but couldn't spot Earl and the Humvee. He slowed to a crawl and listened. An engine sputtered, trying to catch, somewhere back the way he'd come. He started to turn. Then the engine caught and roared to life, so much so that Seb thought it might flood.

Tires spun, and the Humvee came racing up on his right. Its side was caved in between the front and back doors. The vehicle and its passengers had taken a hell of a hit. The turret was gone.

Where's Malcolm?

Earl was shaken but not stirred. "Move, ya dumb idiot," he yelled out the hole where his window— designed to withstand shrapnel and small arms fire—had been. The Humvee burst past him, the metal tray it was hauling still attached and still carrying the two ATVs, though one had tipped over.

Seb peeked over his shoulder in one last attempt to leave no soldier behind, but Malcolm had vanished without a trace. He gritted his teeth. *Things are going to be a lot harder from here on out.*

He hit the gas and pressed on, the Humvee pulling ahead of him. It was hauling more than just the ATVs. A cord encircled the back of the cab, looped in through the back windows. Its other end, which Seb couldn't see, extended into the air.

Gunfire resumed. The noise came from above him.

"No goddamn way!" Slack-jawed and sucking in a breath, Seb followed the cord up higher and higher as the Humvee clunked and clanged its way toward a bottleneck, their only possible road out.

"Where'd he get the fucking parachute?" He shook his head, trying to snap out of his stupor and concentrate on driving. But with Malcolm parasailing above him, toting a massive machine gun like an eighties Schwarzenegger hero, he thought he'd seen the unbelievable for a third time that day.

Let's hope the fourth is us making it out of here alive.

Angelique made it past the tentacle and into the narrowing path, while Malcolm kept the beast bleeding. Sly made it through next. The Humvee slowed, but only a little, jerking forward every time Malcolm started to fall.

Seb shifted, then shifted again, the Charger's electronic shifting mechanism—already set to near-optimal performance—made even better with his precision timing through manual shifting built into his steering wheel. Earl was waiting for him to pass. The Charger earned its name, bulleting forward like a first-down running back. Only this running back had seven hundred seven horsepower behind it. Seb hoped it was enough, considering the defensive line was a brick wall.

In a matter of seconds, Seb passed under the creature and was in sight of Sly's bumper. But he slowed then, watching in his side mirror to see if Earl and Malcolm made it through okay.

"Oh no . . ."

In his efforts to raise the tentacle out of the caravan's path, Malcolm had placed the appendage directly into his own flight trajectory. He fired away at the tentacle, flitting and jerking as if in the throes of a spasm, but it would not return to its cave.

Seb closed his eyes a half second and said a prayer.

The Humvee braked hard. Malcolm plummeted to the earth, his arms outstretched, one hand still holding the weapon. Seb couldn't watch. What was Earl thinking? Paralyzing Malcolm wouldn't be better than killing him.

But Earl never let the vehicle get too slow, and when he slammed on the gas, Seb saw the genius in the crazy cracker's plan. The Humvee tugged Malcolm forward. The degree of the angle created by Malcolm, the Humvee, and the ground increased from thirty-five degrees, to forty-eight degrees, to sixty-six degrees, but not before Malcolm, parachute and all, had sailed safely under that looming evil.

He floated closer and higher, his face as serene as an angel's. Behind him, the tentacle floundered against the dry land, flicking at the air once or twice before falling limp. Then twitching. Then rising.

The creature moved slowly at first, but its arm was gaining speed faster than Seb had seen any part of it move yet, excepting the black gunk it spat. He buried his palms into his horn, but he was already too late.

As if filmed by his side mirror, its lens angled up from the IROC's impact to capture all, Seb could only watch as the tentacle whipped through Malcolm's parachute and swatted the soldier in midair. Its momentum sent a burst of wind howling around the Hellcat.

Yet its touch was comparatively gentle, not batting Malcolm like a tennis ball but wrapping him in a lover's embrace.

It took hold of him, drawing him toward the mountains, snapping his tether to the Humvee as if it were an old elastic. Malcolm struggled as the narrower end of the appendage coiled tighter. His gun fell to the ground, useless.

From below, Earl fired up from the parked Humvee, but his shots were wide, likely for fear of hitting Malcolm. Seb added a few rounds from his peashooter, but from his distance, he doubted they had any effect.

Malcolm was over the mountains, soon to be out of range entirely. But he never made it to the thing's mouth, wherever it hid. The tentacle constricted like an anaconda, tighter and tighter around him until it squished him into human jam.

This seemed to annoy the creature. It shrieked and snapped its arm straight out, raining droplets of blood and gore over the dirt. Like a spear, it stabbed under the Humvee just as Earl got it moving again. The Humvee flipped into the air, a flapjack spinning out of the frying pan but about to crash down into the fire.

The ATVs fell to the ground. Seb couldn't see if Earl had dove clear. The Humvee broke against the earth like a soda can beneath a tire. Nothing moved.

Except the tentacle, which turned toward him, eyeless yet somehow seeing. He punched the gas.

Up ahead, Angelique was having her own problems. Bullets sprayed from the buggy. She was holding what looked like an Uzi. The filter of small rounds gave her enough room to squeeze under a sixth tentacle, and the spike atop her roll bars caught and slashed open the beast's skin, forcing a shriek from some new location up ahead and to the left, with an outpouring of what looked like banana pudding from the wound. It coated Sly's Chevelle and Seb's Charger as they sped beneath it.

"She's taking too many risks." Seb hit his fist against the steering wheel. "Another goddamn martyr." Earl, Malcolm, Helen, Red, and probably Skeeter—they had lost too many, and he had only himself to blame. He snarled. It wasn't the time for self-pity.

Angelique was blazing a trail.

The path had shriveled to less than thirty yards across, giving them not a lot of room to maneuver. When the seventh tentacle crashed down a dozen yards or so in front of her, Angelique couldn't avoid it. She slammed into the beast head-on, her front spikes jabbing the rubbery purple skin and snapping under it. The tentacle rolled against and under her tires, sending the buggy's ass end flipping over its front end like a coin, jettisoning her high into the air. Her spiraling momentum carried her over the tentacle even as it rose again, allowing Sly and Seb to pass beneath it.

Somehow, Angelique landed on her wheels, bouncing like a moon rover. She skidded and drove over the rocks at the path's edge but soon regained control. Pulling toward the middle of the path, Angelique rode next to Sly. She was okay. She was really, truly, miraculously okay. Seb was so happy, he might have—

Sly shot out her tire.

Angelique fishtailed then began to roll. After going side over side like a tumbleweed, the buggy came to a stop, belly up. Angelique hung upside down, still belted into her seat. She wrenched her helmet off and tossed it aside.

Seb stopped alongside the buggy and pushed open his passenger-side door. "Come on!" he yelled, beckoning her with his hand. "Hurry!"

She didn't move fast enough for his tastes, so he slung himself out to help her. As he circled the Charger, Angelique scrambled from the wreck on her knees and elbows. Seb hurried to her and helped her up.

"Go!" she yelled so ferociously that he was momentarily startled. "Keep going, you idiot!"

Seb didn't listen. After checking if she could stand, he took stock of her as quickly as he could. She seemed whole. Other than a scraped elbow and a limp he couldn't attribute to any noticeable injury, she seemed okay. After all she'd been through, she was lucky to be alive.

His arm around her shoulders, Seb hustled her to his car. He was about to help her into it when she froze, refusing or no longer able to move forward.

Tears welled in her eyes. "Save her," she whispered just before being jerked backward out of his grasp. The black sticky goop drew taut and snatched her toward an open maw bigger than that of any prehistoric monster Seb could recall. He saw no teeth or tongue, just an indeterminable depth filled with wriggling stalactites and screams and reeking of infection and decay. It swallowed Angelique whole.

Seb slammed the door shut. "I'll kill him. I swear to god I'm gonna kill him!"

He ran around the car and jumped behind the wheel as Skeeter roared by in his F-150. Its fender was missing, and its white paint was coated with grime. "Kill him!" Seb yelled. "Kill that motherfucker!"

Skeeter honked his horn and floored the gas pedal in answer. Message received.

The eighth tentacle slammed down behind Skeeter, forcing Seb, who'd been racing to catch up, to jerk the wheel hard. He ran alongside the appendage, the roadside rapidly approaching. He hoped the tentacle wasn't longer than the stretch of road left.

It was.

"Fuck!" He couldn't get past it and had to turn around. He grabbed his guns and steadied the wheel with his knee.

"Look out!" a man yelled.

"Earl?" Something flashed across his path several yards ahead. It wasn't Earl.

Instinct made him turn away from the tentacle just as it exploded in an inferno of fire and pudding. With a series of clinks, shrapnel stabbed into his hood and splintered his windshield. A tire once belonging to an ATV, now in pieces, bounced off his hood. He skidded to a halt, ducking as flames leapt through the open window.

As the air cooled and the smoke cleared, a bodiless tentacle flapped on the road. Slowly, it began to shrivel, withering in a matter of moments much as a corpse would over a decade. After a minute, it stopped moving altogether.

His passenger door opened, and Earl got in. Blood caked the big man's nostrils and ran from one ear. His stomach was a round mound of filth and sweat. His cheek was scraped, and dots of blood soaked through his T-shirt. He was missing a sneaker.

"The way out's that way." Earl pointed through the gap made by the explosion.

Seb took his foot off the brake. "What the hell just happened?"

"Grenades," Earl said flatly. "Malcolm brought more than just his assault rifle in that combat vehicle. I just wish he'd brought along some RPGs." He rubbed his hands together. "Now, can we please get the hell out of here?"

Seb shook his head and drove. "Sly . . . he killed Angelique."

Earl sighed and shook his head. He sniffed and stared straight ahead.

"How is he here? I mean, come on. You were a medic. How can he still be alive?"

Earl didn't say anything as the Charger rolled through a swamp of creature fluids. After a long silence, he said, "Let's just worry about getting out of here. We'll worry about all that other stuff later . . . if there is a later."

Seb straightened in his seat. "We've come too far to die now. Besides, I counted eight of those . . . tentacles. If this thing's, like, I don't know . . . an octopus or something, are we past it?"

"How can you be sure it was eight? That thing moves. Maybe you're double counting." Seb checked his rearview and the little girl resting so quietly, so peaceably, in his back seat as the whole world around them went to hell. He pursed his lips. *I hope you're worth it, kid.*

"She's worth it," Earl said, as if reading his thoughts. "Skeeter's up ahead with that asshole, Sly. We've got to help him if we can. Step on it."

Seb obliged. He had a score to settle with Sly, that tire-shooting son of a bitch.

Catching up proved easier than Seb had thought. A ninth tentacle—shattering Seb's theory and his wishful thinking—blocked the path forward, and Sly's Chevelle was stopped in front of it. Skeeter's truck was fighting against the pull of that black nastiness clinging like a spiderweb to its bed.

Seb handed Earl a pistol, and they both took aim at the black goop. Earl fired to his gun clicked empty. So did Seb. Neither was able to detach that gunk from the F-150. They were out of bullets and out of options.

Skeeter was not. He twisted in his seat and butted out the cab's back window, then pointed a shotgun at the inky mess, all the while keeping his foot on the gas. It took only one shot before he was barreling forward, the F-150 bounding out of control.

Skeeter hit the brake then started to back up. He

angled the truck toward the Chevelle, which was slowly creeping away from the tentacle, as if Sly thought a sudden movement might wake it.

Seb and Earl exchanged a knowing look. Skeeter's intentions were clear. He was going to ram the fucker.

Sly must have known it, too, because he slammed down on the accelerator, but the Chevelle was no match for the F-150. The two vehicles collided with the grinding of metal, the Chevelle's bumper entangling with the mess that had been the F-150's grille. The Chevelle lurched forward, Sly thrown against his dashboard. Slowly, gradually, Skeeter pushed the car's front end into the white gelatinous underside of the tentacle before Sly could recover and turn.

Trapped, the murderer shot through his back window in a desperate attempt to shake Skeeter off him. Firing his gun until it, too, shot empty, Sly hollered and cursed. Still, Skeeter kept pushing even as the black mucus slapped against the pickup's door, jacking it right off its hinges. Skeeter hardly seemed to notice, his face twisted in rage, intent on killing Sly for real that time. The door disappeared into a cave to the left, really close. Too close.

The smell of refuse and gangrene filled the air, clinging to a heavy mist, thick enough to have a taste that made a pile of horseshit seem appetizing. Seb couldn't see the rest of the creature, but he could sense it. To his left, to his right, it was all around him. He knew with every fiber of his being that the creature could see them.

He steeled himself. "We have to go."

"How?" Earl asked. "It's blocking the road."

"Do you have any more grenades?"

"Nope."
"Bullets?"
"No."
"Anything?"
Earl paused. "Nope."
Seb jolted. "Skeeter's shotgun!"

In an almost uncanny coincidence, the black goop returned with lightning speed, perhaps going for the very thing Seb was after. Skeeter screamed. The beast tore him from the cab, slinging him toward itself. In a blink, Skeeter was gone, his agony echoing through the dark caverns all around them.

Though the truck was idling, no longer pushing the Chevelle into the tentacle, the sponge-like flesh kept absorbing the car into itself, dissolving rubber, leather, and metal indiscriminately. Sly dove into the back seat and was crawling out of the broken rear windshield onto the trunk.

"Was Skeeter holding the shotgun when that thing got him?" Earl asked.

"We better hope not." Seb watched Sly push himself out the back windshield, slide off the trunk and plop onto the ground. "You get the gun." He clenched his fists. "I'll handle that asshole."

He jumped out of the car and ran at Sly. The psycho-junkie was still on the ground when Seb reached him. All the rage and violence that had gotten him into so much trouble, time and time again, poured out of Seb, and he kicked wildly.

"This is for Angelique." He grunted and buried a kick in Sly's armpit. "This is for Mary." He stomped on Sly's forehead. "This is for Skeeter. This is for Helen, and this is for me!"

With every name came another kick. On the last one, loosely aimed at Sly's ribs, Sly caught Seb's leg and tripped him. Bruised and bloody, Sly nevertheless got up first. He pulled out a knife.

"Gutting you will be so much more satisfying than that old bitch." Sly giggled. "And when you're gone, who will protect the girl?" He licked his lips in a way that instantly made Seb want to rip them off his face.

The bullet wound in Sly's head puckered like an asshole. It had scabbed over, the blood having clotted and the wound beginning to heal, before Seb had stomped it open. Seb had almost forgotten how Angelique had shot out half of Sly's brain. With the wound reopened, he thought again how the child-molesting sicko had no right—or reason—to be alive.

And the exit wound should have sealed the deal. Seb couldn't see that but was sure he didn't want to. *He's got no business walking. When I put him down, I'll make sure he stays down.*

"I think I'll bring her back the way we came, then have my way with her over and over again at the tent." Sly grinned lecherously, all toothy like a vampire hovering over a bare neck. "I'll have her all to myself now. I don't think the creature will mind my going back. Do you?"

He's stalling. Seb dusted himself off. *He knows he can't take me but thinks the creature will take out one of us soon enough. He's banking on me being next.*

"Drop it," Earl said, Skeeter's shotgun tucked under his arm.

"Earl," Seb whispered. "Get back in the car. That black shit—"

"Don't worry." Earl walked up beside him. "I got your . . . oh shit—"

Earl's face contorted into a mask of agony. His skin turned purple, his eyes widened, and his forehead rained sweat. "Here," he managed through gritted teeth. He tossed Seb the shotgun just as the beast yanked him out of sight.

The gun twirled through the air. As Seb reached up to catch it, a knife jabbed him in the side. Its burn was familiar, almost as if Sly had stabbed him exactly where he'd been shot.

Not almost.

As Sly pulled the knife free, Seb caught the gun and slammed the barrel into Sly's jaw. It sent the junkie tumbling backward, head over heels. After rolling a bit, he landed on his stomach.

Seb pressed the shotgun barrel against Sly's skull.

Sly sneered. "Go on. Do it."

"You ain't worth the bullet."

Sly began to laugh, but his laughter soon faltered, replaced by a look of recognition, then terror, then pleas for help.

Then screaming.

The toe of his sneaker had dug into the tentacle. It was pulling him in slowly, dissolving him inch by inch.

"Help me!" he screamed. He clawed at the dust, his fingers digging grooves into the earth. All the while he bellowed in pain.

It warmed Seb's heart. Vengeance was so much more satisfying than court justice. Wanting to see it through, but realizing the error in doing so, he hustled to the car. As impossible as it seemed, a friend was waiting, his tongue lolling, stretching his paws in the dirt. "You've got to be kidding me."

Juke tilted his head. He pattered over to the Charger and whimpered.

"All right, buddy. Get in." Seb opened the back door, and Juke hopped in and lay down beside Mary.

Seb slid behind the wheel and drove straight up to the tentacle, searching for a solid pinkish-purple section. When he found one, he blasted the shit out of it with Skeeter's weapon, hanging half out the window so that he could manage the recoil with both hands. By then, Sly had already gone silent. The creature shrieked. Juke howled in response.

As the creature pulled away, Seb sped beneath it. Immediately, the sky filled with darkness, two more skyscraper tentacles rising out of new holes in the rock. He groaned. "Why couldn't there be only eight? Fuck this." He sighed and checked on his passengers in his rearview. "Hold on back there."

He shifted to fourth, fifth, sixth, seventh, then topped off at eighth gear, his engine's pitch rising to a beautiful crescendo. He picked up the injection device. The road ahead darkened, as if the skies were about to unleash their fury.

In a way, they were.

Here goes nothing. Seb pressed the trigger button. Nitrous flowed through a tube and into the cylinder. The engine's roar became a whine, and the car jumped forward. Arms straight, his back pressed flat against his seat, Seb pushed the Charger to go faster than he'd ever driven anything. One fifty. One sixty. One eighty.

He worried his tires' traction wouldn't hold. He worried more that he wouldn't be fast enough. Thump after thump came from behind him, like a whole forest of trees tumbling down. One limb smacked so close to his taillights that his back tires left the ground and his front end slapped dirt. But he barely lost a beat, the car touching down again, spurring him faster and faster forward, over two hundred miles per hour, Seb never taking his foot off the gas.

CHAPTER 8

UP AHEAD, DAYLIGHT. A sky without tentacles. Freedom.

And still he raced forward. "No, no, no!" The path widened, and for a moment, Seb thought he'd somehow been turned around. Behind him were the mountains, and they circled him on the left and the right. In front of him, a desert wasteland. He saw no sign of the creature or any of its many parts.

He laughed. "It's not the same. Can't be. We're safe. Safe."

Metal glinted somewhere on the empty horizon. As his engine sputtered, the contents of his fuel tank burned away, he slowed down. He'd been clenched up so tightly that his shoulders ached. As his speed dipped below a hundred, he allowed himself a modicum of relaxation. His shoulders dropped from beside his ears. The breath he'd been holding whistled through his teeth.

The grooves of the steering wheel left imprints across his palms. Seb flexed his fingers and squinted, straining to make out the source of the shimmer.

It was a building of some sort with a small covered area. And under the covered part—

"Fuel pumps! A gas station!"

Juke sat up at Seb's sudden outburst. He poked his head between the front seats, his tongue still lolling. The poor animal must have been exhausted and dehydrated—not to mention terrified—given the distance he'd covered and danger through which he'd run. But he seemed in good spirits in spite of it all.

Seb put an arm around the coyote. "We made it, bud. We actually made it!" He ruffled the animal's fur and laughed. He kept laughing long and hard before he realized he was crying.

Movement came from the back seat. With her hands balled into fists, Mary wiped the sleep from her eyes. "I'm thirsty," she said, her voice a raspy whisper.

"You're awake?" Seb tried to temper his excitement. He willed away his stupid grin. "How are you feeling?"

Mary ignored the question. "Where's Angel?"

The girl sounded younger than her years, and Seb realized it was the first time he'd heard her speak. Then he realized he'd been thrown into a foreign and perhaps scarier circumstance than driving through monster-dominated "mountains of madness," as Sly had called them. He had a little girl to care for. He knew as much about raising children as he did space exploration. And reaching her, well, Mary might as well have been on another planet.

Worse still, he had to explain what had happened to the family who had cared for Mary for god knew how long. A pang shot through his stomach. His chin quivered. "She, uh . . . well, she didn't make it, kid." He stared blankly out the front windshield. "I'm sorry. It's just us now."

"What do you mean?" Mary pressed her face against the window. "Where are the others?" Her fingers left prints on the glass. "Where are we?"

"We made it through the mountains." Seb smiled sadly, thinking of how they'd beaten that monster, remembering how much it had cost. "We're free."

Mary scrunched up her nose and stuck out her lower lip. She kicked the back of the passenger seat. "Where. Is. Angel?"

"She's gone, Mary. They're all gone." He stopped the car, the gas station less than a quarter mile away. His instincts told him to keep going, but that other part of him, that part he saved for Gemma, told him he should comfort the girl.

He put his arm around the passenger seat and turned. "I know it's hard, but now that we're out of there, maybe we can find your real parents . . . a relative or something. Until then, you can stay with us. I've got a girlfriend, Gemma, who I'm sure you're gonna—"

Mary clasped her hands over her ears and screamed.

Seb winced and turned away. He wondered if something might be wrong with the girl, something he wasn't equipped to handle, and he instantly hated himself for thinking it. She looked to be twelve but was acting half that. One thing was true, though: he didn't know how to handle her screams. And responsibility had never been his strong suit.

He bit down and endured the shrill pitch until Mary fell silent. Painful as it was, it was nothing compared to that creature's shriek. After shifting into drive, he drove the remainder of the way to the pumps.

The gas station looked deserted. The pumps were layered with dirt and grime. He got out of the car and tucked a pistol in his waistband. He knew the weapon was empty, true, but he owned the market share on that knowledge.

The ground was more of the same: dry, cracked earth, nothing moving, nothing alive. He studied it for tracks—human, vehicle, or otherwise—but saw none other than his own.

With his sleeve, he wiped away the filth covering the gas prices. "Thirty-two cents a gallon!" He couldn't believe what he was seeing. Gas prices had never been that low in his lifetime. And even better, the pumps appeared to be operational, so long as the gasoline hadn't gone and dried up like the rest of the place.

Seb snickered. *You just drove by something way bigger than Bigfoot, and it's gas prices you can't believe?* He shook his head, laughing quietly, the stress of the day giving way to the euphoria of being inexplicably yet truly alive.

The gas station itself presented more questions than it answered. Advertisements for cigarettes and colas, brands known and unknown, covered the windows. The prices made him want to fill up his trunk and set up a black-market shop elsewhere. An ice cabinet sat along the front of the building. An old pink Schwinn, complete with a basket over its rear wheel and tassels hanging from its handlebars, lay tipped over beside a busted barrel. Unlike everything else, the bike wasn't covered in dust.

He squinted at the door, a dual-sided open-and-closed sign turned to the latter message staring back at him. And above it, a pair of eyes behind glasses peered out.

Seb tapped his Hellcat's hood. "I'm going inside. Stay here."

He hadn't taken more than a few steps beyond the front of his car when he heard its door opening behind him and Mary getting out. He turned and gave her a wry smile as Juke slid out silently beside her.

"I thought I told you to—"

Mary kicked him in the shin. "That's for leaving Angel behind, you jerk."

Seb hopped on one foot, his shin stinging with sharp, concentrated pain. The little girl had quite the soccer leg.

"Why, you ungrateful—"

Juke bared his fangs and snapped at Seb. The animal clearly hadn't meant to bite, his fangs closing several inches away from Seb's hand, but the warning was received loud and clear.

"Okay, okay," he said as Mary and Juke continued past him toward the station's front door. He waved grandiosely. "After you."

A smooth black object lay on the ground behind where Mary had been standing. "Aw, hell no." Seb placed his hands on his hips, staring at it and knowing what it was, not ready to see its magic window facedown in the sand.

"Haven't you done enough?" He scooped up the small toy that had once served as a drug dealer's glass eye. "What? You just want to torment me some more?"

He turned the 8 Ball over in his hand. *You may rely on it.*

"Oh yeah?" Seb cocked back his arm. "Well, fuck

you!" He launched the glass eye back toward the mountains from which he'd escaped. "I'm done listening to anything or anyone but myself."

As he stepped inside the store, Seb heard a series of clicks. He threw his arms up. Only then did he register the guns and the throng of people holding them, hiding behind sparsely stocked racks.

The bespectacled man whose eyes Seb had seen through the door had moved behind a counter, exposing an upper body clad in a bowling shirt with a name tag that read Leo across his chest. The rifle he pointed at Seb, old-fashioned as it was, didn't shake in his hands. Even if Seb's gun were loaded, he would never have gotten a shot off.

"Whoa there," he said, keeping his hands where everyone could see them. "We were just looking to fill up, maybe grab some snacks, and be on our way." He stepped backward, his butt pressing against the doors, which had swung closed behind him.

"Don't move," Leo said, no emotion in his voice. His stern frown and hard gaze demanded compliance.

Seb froze. Mary and Juke pattered around the store, no one paying them any attention.

Leo nodded with his rifle. "Who are you? How'd you get here?"

"Nobody special." Seb grinned sheepishly. "I don't know what I walked in on here, and I don't want to. If you'll just be letting me go on my way, I'll—"

"I know him," blurted a young woman in overalls, her hair tied in a ponytail. She riffled through several newspapers in her hands as she approached the counter.

Seb hoped she would step into the rifle's path, even

if just for a moment, long enough for him to back out the door and dash for the car. He'd come back for the girl and the coyote, too, but he'd do it armed to the teeth.

"He's the thief!" The woman slammed one of the newspapers on the counter, then jabbed it with her finger. "Here."

"I'll be damned," Leo muttered. His gun's barrel drooped, and he looked away. "Shootout near Rio," he read aloud. "Five dead in black-market deal gone bad. Suspect missing."

Seb saw his chance to escape, but curiosity kept him rooted to the linoleum floor. He lowered his arms but made no dumb moves for his gun. He took a step toward the man. "May I have a look?"

"Have at it," Leo said, smiling and throwing his rifle's strap over his shoulder. "Sorry about all the guns. With that newfangled car you're driving, Sammy back there thought you might be a cop."

"Sorry," someone shouted from the back of the store.

"Some of the others thought you might be something worse." Leo guffawed. "Looks like you're famous like the rest of us."

Seb stared at the newspaper. Sure, he'd made the front page, but the newspaper itself struck him as funny. Fading, its ink a duller version of its former self. The chronicled deal gone bad had been only a few days prior, yet for some reason, the paper looked ages old.

A couple days ago, right? Seb scratched his chin. *Couldn't have been more than a week.* Before he could turn the memory over in his mind, the woman slammed another newspaper over the first one. The journal, the *San Bernardino Gazette*, was brown and brittle with age. The ink had turned a bluish hue.

"The girl," the woman said, slamming a palm down on the paper. "I bet that's her. No picture, though."

"Now, Elsa, just because she's Asian—"

Elsa crossed her arms. "How many coolies you know out there?"

Leo tsked. "In California? Ain't you never heard of Chinatown?"

"And the scars?"

The two continued to argue, but Seb blocked them out. His focus was on the article, an account of a twelve-year-old Chinese-American girl who had set fire to an entire apartment complex, barricading the doors and trapping everyone—including her parents—inside. The paper explained that the little girl herself was critically injured when embers from the roaring blaze sparked against the gasoline she'd spilled on her clothes and skin. Witnesses claimed that on her way to the hospital, the little girl was laughing.

Another article talked about "Ol' Blue Eyes" doing another run at the Sands. *Ol' Blue Eyes?*

Seb turned around to see Mary staring up at him, a five-cent lighter in her hand, a devilish grin on her face. He looked at the year on the paper—1960— then at Mary, the beginning of an idea forming that he dismissed just as quickly.

He chuckled nervously. "No . . . " The thought that the girl was somehow his elder, that she hadn't aged a day in more than half a century, was too fantastical to fathom, even after all he'd seen that day.

Or was that yesterday?

"It still doesn't explain how they got here," a teenage boy called from the encroaching crowd.

Leo stopped bickering with Elsa. He turned to Seb. "That's true. How did you get here?"

"You mean, how'd we make it through the mountains with something trying to kill us every damn step of the way?"

Leo nodded. The others drew closer.

"Wasn't easy. I mean, it seemed like everywhere I turned, another tentacle was slamming down around me." Seb's eyebrows formed a mountain peak over his nose. His heart sank, and his mouth went bone dry. Leo's words were registering. Had everything he'd just done and all the deaths that accompanied it . . . had it all been for nothing?

Carlo's words echoed in his head. *There are far worse places than this.*

"Wait . . . " Never before had he been so afraid to ask a question. "Don't tell me. Does that thing have this place surrounded, too?"

"We don't know nothing about no tentacles," Elsa said.

Seb's tension ebbed. He let out a cleansing breath. "Good, good. I can't tell you how much of a relief that is."

"But we're surrounded, all right," Leo added. "How'd you get past the Wing Dings?"

Seb's mouth dropped open. "Wing Dings?"

Leo threw his hands up. "Sorry, that's just what Sammy calls them. I mean, those flying devils."

Seb tried out the words. "Flying . . . devils?"

"Yeah," Leo said, nodding. "You know, big flying blood-sucking bastards straight out of some Dark Ages tableau. Real mean motherfuckers, scooping up anyone who gets too close to those mountains?"

Seb stood silent, stunned. "Just lucky, I guess." He didn't like what he was hearing. Flying devils? After all that had happened, it wasn't so much hard to believe but hard to take in. Could he really be trapped all over again, surrounded by some new version of hell with an entirely different form of evil to outrun and outwit? Had the whole world gone crazy overnight, or was this nightmare a horror reserved solely for him?

He huffed out a breath as the unfairness of it all filled him with rage. He took in the crowd, about ten people in all.

Ten able-bodied drivers.

He leaned over the counter. "Do you have cars?"

"Yeah," Leo said, stepping back. "We all have cars. More than we need, even. But they ain't good for nothing with those demons flying straight into your windshield. They swarm you, like in that Hitchcock movie."

"You have guns?"

Elsa snickered. She threw a thumb at the wall behind her. It was plastered with artillery.

A wicked smile that he couldn't hide ran across Seb's lips. He was getting out of there. He was getting back to Gemma, even if he had to use up every last person in that gas station.

Leo's face paled. "Just what are you thinking, mister?"

Seb gritted his teeth. "I'm thinking of getting out . . . of getting all of us out. I've got a plan, but we've all got to be willing to work together." He scanned the terrified crowd. "Now, who's with me?"

THE END?

Not if you want to dive into more of Crystal Lake Publishing's Tales from the Darkest Depths!

Website: www.crystallakepub.com/
Amazon: amazon.com/author/crystalpublishing

ABOUT THE AUTHOR

Jason Parent is an author of horror, thrillers, mysteries, science fiction and dark humor, though his many novels, novellas, and short stories tend to blur the boundaries between genres. From his EPIC and eFestival Independent Book Award finalist first novel, *What Hides Within*, to his widely applauded police procedural/supernatural thriller, *Seeing Evil*, to his fast and furious sci-fi horror, *The Apocalypse Strain*, Jason's work has won him praise from both critics and fans of diverse genres alike. He currently lives in Rhode Island, surrounded by chewed furniture thanks to his corgi and mini Aussie pups.

Dear reader,

It makes our day to know you reached the end of our book. Thank you so much. This is why we do what we do every single day.

Please take a moment to leave a review on Amazon, Goodreads, or anywhere else readers visit. Reviews go a long way to helping an author, and will help us to continue publishing quality books. You can also share a photo of yourself on social holding this book with the hashtag #IGotMyCLPBook!

Thank you again for taking the time to journey with Crystal Lake Publishing.

Website:
www.crystallakepub.com

Amazon:
amazon.com/author/crystalpublishing

Twitter:
https://twitter.com/crystallakepub

Facebook:
https://www.facebook.com/Crystallakepublishing/

Instagram:
https://www.instagram.com/crystal_lake_publishing/

Patreon:
https://www.patreon.com/CLP

Join the Crystal Lake journey by signing up for our newsletter and receive three eBooks for free: http://eepurl.com/xfuKP

Or check out other Crystal Lake Publishing books for more Tales from the Darkest Depths. You can also subscribe to Crystal Lake Classics, where you'll receive fortnightly info on all our books, starting all the way back at the beginning, with personal notes on every release. Or join our interactive community of authors and readers on Patreon for exclusive content and behind the scenes access, bonus short stories, polls, interviews and, if you're interested, author support.

Since its founding in August 2012, Crystal Lake Publishing has quickly become one of the world's leading publishers of Dark Fiction and Horror books in print, eBook, and audio formats.

While we strive to present only the highest quality fiction and entertainment, we also endeavour to support authors along their writing journey. We offer our time and experience in non-fiction projects, as well as author mentoring and services, at competitive prices.

With several Bram Stoker Award wins and many other wins and nominations, Crystal Lake Publishing puts integrity, honor, and respect at the forefront of our publishing operations.

We strive for each book and outreach program we spearhead to not only entertain and touch or comment on issues that affect our readers, but also to strengthen and support the Dark Fiction field and its authors.

Not only do we find and publish authors we believe are destined for greatness, but we strive to work with men and woman who endeavour to be decent human beings who care more for others than themselves, while still being hard working, driven, and passionate artists and storytellers.

Crystal Lake Publishing is and will always be a beacon of what passion and dedication, combined with overwhelming teamwork and respect, can accomplish. We endeavour to know each and every one of our readers, while building personal relationships with our authors, reviewers, bloggers, podcasters, bookstores, and libraries.

We will be as trustworthy, forthright, and transparent as any business can be, while also keeping most of the headaches away from our authors, since it's our job to solve the problems so they can stay in a creative mind. Which of course also means paying our authors.

We do not just publish books, we present to you worlds within your world, doors within your mind, from talented authors who sacrifice so much for a moment of your time.

There are some amazing small presses out there, and through collaboration and open forums we will continue to support other presses in the goal of helping authors and showing the world what quality small presses are capable of accomplishing. No one wins when a small press goes down, so we will always be there to support hardworking, legitimate presses and their authors. We don't see Crystal Lake as the best press out there, but we will always strive to be the best, strive to be the most interactive and grateful, and even blessed press around. No matter what happens over time, we will also take our mission very seriously while appreciating where we are and enjoying the journey.

What do we offer our authors that they can't do for themselves through self-publishing?

We are big supporters of self-publishing (especially hybrid publishing), if done with care, patience, and planning. However, not every author has the time or inclination to do market research, advertise, and set up book launch strategies. Although a lot of authors are successful in doing it all, strong small presses will always be there for the authors who just want to do what they do best: write.

What we offer is experience, industry knowledge, contacts and trust built up over years. And due to our strong brand and trusting fanbase, every Crystal Lake Publishing book comes with weight of respect. In time our fans begin to trust our judgment and will try a new author purely based on our support of said author.

With each launch we strive to fine-tune our approach, learn from our mistakes, and increase our reach. We continue to assure our authors that we're here for them and that we'll carry the weight of the launch and dealing with third parties while they focus on their strengths—be it writing, interviews, blogs, signings, etc.

We also offer several mentoring packages to authors that include knowledge and skills they can use in both traditional and self-publishing endeavours.

We look forward to launching many new careers.

This is what we believe in. What we stand for. This will be our legacy.

Welcome to Crystal Lake Publishing—Tales from the Darkest Depths

www.ingramcontent.com/pod-product-compliance
Lightning Source LLC
LaVergne TN
LVHW011843060526
838200LV00054B/4149